D0010365

THE INVENTION OF SOUND

ALSO BY CHUCK PALAHNIUK

MT. PLEASANT PUBLIC LIBRARY
MT. PLEASANT. IOWA
DISCARD

THE
INVENTION
OF SOUND

CHUCK
PALAHNIUK

GRAND CENTRAL
PUBLISHING

NEW YORK   BOSTON

This book is a work of fiction. Names, characters, places, and incidents are the product of the author's imagination or are used fictitiously. Any resemblance to actual events, locales, or persons, living or dead, is coincidental.

Copyright © 2020 by Chuck Palahniuk

Cover art and design by Tree Abraham
Cover copyright © 2020 by Hachette Book Group, Inc.

Hachette Book Group supports the right to free expression and the value of copyright. The purpose of copyright is to encourage writers and artists to produce the creative works that enrich our culture.

The scanning, uploading, and distribution of this book without permission is a theft of the author's intellectual property. If you would like permission to use material from the book (other than for review purposes), please contact permissions@hbgusa.com. Thank you for your support of the author's rights.

Grand Central Publishing
Hachette Book Group
1290 Avenue of the Americas, New York, NY 10104
grandcentralpublishing.com
twitter.com/grandcentralpub

First edition: September 2020

Grand Central Publishing is a division of Hachette Book Group, Inc. The Grand Central Publishing name and logo is a trademark of Hachette Book Group, Inc.

The publisher is not responsible for websites (or their content) that are not owned by the publisher.

The Hachette Speakers Bureau provides a wide range of authors for speaking events. To find out more, go to www.hachettespeakersbureau.com or call (866) 376-6591.

Library of Congress Cataloging-in-Publication Data

Names: Palahniuk, Chuck, author.
Title: The invention of sound / Chuck Palahniuk.
Description: New York : Grand Central Publishing, 2020.
Identifiers: LCCN 2020008872 (print) | LCCN 2020008873 (ebook) | ISBN 9781538718001 (hardcover) | ISBN 9781538717998 (ebook)
Subjects: GSAFD: Suspense fiction. | Mystery fiction.
Classification: LCC PS3566.A4554 I575 2020 (print) | LCC PS3566.A4554 (ebook) | DDC 813/.54—dc23
LC record available at https://lccn.loc.gov/2020008872
LC ebook record available at https://lccn.loc.gov/2020008873

ISBNs: 978-1-5387-1800-1 (hardcover), 978-1-5387-1799-8 (ebook)

Printed in the United States of America

LSC-C

10 9 8 7 6 5 4 3 2 1

THE INVENTION OF SOUND

Keep Telling Yourself It's Only a Movie

PART ONE:

FORGET US OUR TRESPASSES

An ambulance wailed through the streets, and every dog howled. Pekingese and border collies alike. German shepherds and Boston terriers and whippets. Mongrels and purebreds. Dalmatians, Doberman pinschers, poodles, basset hounds, and bulldogs. Herding dogs and lapdogs. House pets and strays. Mixed-breed and pedigreed, they howled together as the siren went past.

And for that long going-by they were all members of the same pack. And the howls of all dogs, they were one howl. And that howl was so loud it drowned out the siren. Until the sound that had united them all had vanished, and yet their howling sustained itself.

For no dog could bear to abandon, first, that rare moment of their communion.

* * *

3

In bed, Jimmy propped himself on one elbow and listened. He asked, "Why?"

Beside him Mitzi stirred. She reached a glass of wine off the floor and asked, "Why what?"

In the office building across the street, a single window glowed. Framed behind it, a man stared at a computer screen, his face washed by the shifting light of moving images. This light danced on his eyeglasses and shimmered on the tears running down his cheek.

Not just outside but in the condos that surrounded them, the baying continued. Among the hairs on Jimmy's damp, drooping penis, a blister festered. It looked ready to burst, a lump swollen with pink-white pus. He asked, "Why do dogs howl like that?"

When she reached over to pick at the lump, it wasn't a disease. Stuck to his skin it was: A pill. Medicine. A loose sleeping pill. An Ambien, she plucked it, put it in her mouth and slugged it down with wine. She answered, "Limbic resonance."

"What's that?" he asked as he slipped out of the bed. A gentleman Jimmy wasn't. A caveman, yes. Barefoot on the polished wood floor, he grabbed an edge of the mattress and yanked it, Mitzi included, off the box spring. Not by her hair, not this time at least, but he dragged her and the mattress across the bedroom to where tall windows looked over the city. "What's limp dick...?"

"Limbic," she said. "Limbic resonance. It's my job." She set her empty wineglass on the windowsill. The grid of streetlights blazed under the chaos of random stars. The howls were dying away. "My job," Mitzi said, "is to make everyone in the whole world scream at the exact same time."

Instead of a lawyer, Foster called his group leader, Robb. The police weren't even real police. They only worked at the airport. As for Foster, he'd only touched the little girl, a crime it was a stretch to call. He was in custody but only in a lunchroom behind the airline ticket counter. Seated on a folding metal chair. Vending machines filled a whole wall. His hand was bleeding from a small crescent-shaped bite mark.

Only one flight, the girl's, had been delayed, to allow time for her to make a statement.

He asked the fake police to return his phone, and he showed them a screen capture. They had to admit there was a resemblance between the man from the web and today's pervert. The pervert who'd been with the little girl. One fake officer, the guy, asked where Foster had gotten the image, but it wasn't as if Foster could really say.

The other fake cop, the lady cop, told him, "The world is full of missing kids. That doesn't give you the right to snatch someone else's."

For his part, Foster wanted to ask about his checked baggage. His flight for Denver had long since departed. Did they still pull bags if the passenger failed to board? Was his bag being sniffed by bomb-sniffing dogs? Anymore, no city in the world was anywhere you'd want a nice suitcase to go around and around the carousel, unclaimed. Someone without fail would snatch it, pretend to check the luggage tag, disappear out the door.

As for Foster, he'd be okay with a drink. A drink and maybe a couple stitches in his hand.

Before the skirmish, he'd only downed a couple martinis at the concourse bar. He hadn't finished his third when he'd first seen the little girl. What drew his stare was Lucinda's auburn hair, cut shorter than he remembered, so that it only grazed her little shoulders. A girl the same age as Lucinda when she'd disappeared seventeen years before.

At first, he wasn't thinking. That's not how the human heart works. He knew in his head how age progression worked. The pictures on milk cartons. How every year they computer age the kids until adulthood and then only every five years after that. Experts used photos of the mother, her aunts, any female relations, to approximate a new her every five years. There in any supermarket between the Reddi-wip and the half-and-half, Lucinda would be smiling from every carton in the dairy case.

He'd been totally convinced the girl in the airport was Lucinda—until she wasn't.

What raised a red flag was the pervert holding the girl's hand and leading her toward a gate where a flight was boarding. Not missing a beat, Foster had slapped cash on his table and sprinted after them. He'd taken his phone out and was scrolling through stored images. His rogues' gallery. The pixilated faces with unmistakable neck tattoos. Or the full-on face shots of sweating child molesters.

The lowlife, the one leading the little girl, looked to be some Scooby-Doo type. A hemp-headed, shaggy-haired burnout wearing flip-flops. Foster circled, weaving from side to side to get different angles as he snapped photos. Ahead of them the gate agent was checking in passengers at the entrance to a Jetway.

The burnout throwback had presented two tickets, and they were gone through the gate. The last passengers to board.

Out of breath from running, Foster had reached the agent and said, "Call the police."

The agent had stepped into his path, blocking the entrance to the Jetway. She'd signaled to an agent at the podium and held up a hand, saying, "Sir, I need you to stop."

"I'm an investigator." Foster had panted out the words. He'd held up his phone, showing her a grainy screen capture of a shaggy-haired man, his face gaunt, his eyes sunk deep into his skull. Dim and in the distance, he'd heard an announcement for his own flight to begin boarding.

Through the gate area windows, Foster could see the plane. The pilots were framed in the cockpit windows. The ramp crew had stowed the last of the checked luggage and were slamming shut the cargo hatches. They'd be pushing back in another minute.

Foster, he'd shoved past the agent. With more force than he'd intended, he'd strong-armed her so hard she'd tumbled to the floor. His footfalls thundering down the Jetway, he'd shouted, "You don't understand!" To no one in particular, he'd shouted, "He's going to *fuck* her, and he's going to *kill her!*"

A flight attendant had stood ready to close the cabin door, but Foster had elbowed his way past her. He'd stumbled through the first-class section shouting, "That man is a child pornographer!" Waving his phone, he'd shouted, "He destroys kids!"

From his research he knew that child traffickers walk amongst us. They stand beside us at the bank. They sit next to us in restaurants. Foster had scarcely had to scratch the surface of the web before such predators had glommed onto him, sending him their corruption and trying to rope him into their sickening world.

A few passengers had still been standing, waiting in the aisle to take their seats. Last in line had been the girl, still holding the man's hand. They'd looked back when Foster shouted. Everyone had looked, first at him, and then at the man with the girl. Whether it was Foster's blue business suit or his good-boy haircut and egghead glasses, something had thrown the crowd to his aid.

Pointing with his phone, Foster had shouted, "That man is a kidnapper! He runs an international ring for kiddy porn!"

Bleary-eyed and bushy-haired, the accused had uttered only, "Harsh, dude."

When the little girl had started to cry, that seemed to confirm the charge. Potential heroes had unclicked their seat belts and stood, launching themselves and tackling, then dog-piling the caveman lowlife whose muffled protests now nobody could hear. Everyone had been shouting at once, and those people not restraining the burnout had held their phones aloft to shoot video.

Foster had knelt in the airplane aisle and crawled toward the weeping girl, saying, "Take my hand!"

She'd lost hold of the burnout's grip and watched him disappear beneath layers of bodies. Wailing in tears, she'd cried, "Daddy!"

"He's not your daddy," Foster had crooned. "Don't you remember? He kidnapped you from Arlington, Texas." Foster had known the details of the case by heart. "He's not going to hurt you anymore." He'd reached until his large hand had closed over her tiny one.

The girl had shrieked a wordless scream of pain and terror. The press of struggling passengers had held the caveman helplessly buried.

Foster had pulled the little girl into a hug, shushing her and petting her hair as he'd kept repeating, "You're safe. You're safe, now."

At the blurred edge of his vision he'd been aware of passengers holding their phones to record him: this man, some distraught man wearing a navy-blue suit, an ordinary no one, he'd sunk to his knees in the center aisle of the plane grabbing after a little girl in a flowered dress.

An overhead announcement repeated, "This is the pilot speaking. TSA security is en route. Would all passengers please remain in their seats."

The girl had been crying, maybe because Foster was crying. She'd stretched her free hand toward a patch of scruffy pervert hair barely visible under the tumble of bodies.

Foster had taken her tear-stained face between his two hands and brought her innocent brown eyes to meet his. Saying, "You don't have to be his sex slave. Not anymore."

For an instant, everyone had basked in the warm glow of their mutual heroism. In real time, it was all over the internet. Then, on a couple hundred YouTube clips, an air marshal had grabbed Foster in a headlock.

Framed between his hands, the girl's eyes had glazed with a curious, steely resolve.

Choking, he'd assured her, "And you don't have to thank me, Sally."

"My name," the girl had said, "is Cashmere." And she'd turned her tiny head just enough to sink her teeth into the meat of his thumb.

The paramedics had a special name for it. The ones who came to collect the body. They called it "the Fontaine Method," after the high-rise that offered tenants nothing to tie a rope to. A tower of steel-reinforced concrete, with high ceilings broken only by recessed pot lights, what some people called "can" lights. A few units had track lighting.

Stylish, but nothing that would support a person's weight.

A trip to the recycling bins in the building's basement explained a lot. The bin for clear glass was piled full of Patrón bottles and Smirnoff bottles. Her neighbors weren't poor. No one living at the Fontaine ate cat food, except the cats, of course.

Visitors visited rarely. With the exception of the paramedics.

Even now, an ambulance idled at the curb. No lights. No siren. Mitzi watched from the seventeenth floor, from the mattress Jimmy had dragged to the windows. Two men in uniforms bumped a gurney down the building's broad steps and left it sitting on the sidewalk while they opened the rear doors of the ambulance and sat on the tailgate to smoke cigarettes.

The figure on the gurney, covered completely and strapped down, it looked small. A woman, Mitzi guessed. Not a child, because the condo bylaws didn't allow them. More likely an advanced decomp. A few weeks in the California heat could do that, even with the central air-conditioning on high. It could cook a person down like that. Like mummification. Desiccation. The other residents would know who. And whether it was a maid or a strong odor that had summoned the police.

It was the housekeeper, Mitzi knew, who'd found Sharon Tate butchered. It was the housekeeper who'd found Marilyn Monroe cold and naked. It occurred to Mitzi that stumbling across your pregnant boss stabbed to death must be among the worst ways to find yourself out of a job.

Stabbing, Mitzi could write a book about. For example, why some killers kept stabbing for so long. Only the first thrust is intended to inflict pain. The subsequent twenty, thirty, forty stab wounds are to resolve the suffering. It takes as little as one jab or slash to trigger the screaming and bleeding. But so many more are required to make them stop.

Across the street, level with her, a single man sat in his office. A dad-shaped nobody he looked to be, peering into a computer screen she couldn't see. He wore eyeglasses at his desk, in the only office in the building with the lights on.

She'd tried it once, Mitzi had, the Fontaine Method. A simple trick taught by rumor to each new resident. A person simply opened a door. As a metaphor it was poetically sweet. Because there was nowhere else to tie a rope, a person tied it to a doorknob. The soft belt of a terry cloth bathrobe worked well. With one end tied to the knob a person tossed the rest of the belt over the top of the door and fashioned it into a noose. You stood on a chair, kicked the chair aside, and performed your gibbet dance against the door's smooth, painted surface.

12

In olden times, Mitzi knew, no one wanted to curse a tree. So when a hanging took place, people leaned a ladder against a wall and tied a rope to the highest rung. The condemned would stand atop a chair or sit astride a horse. As the chair toppled or the horse bolted, a noose hanging in the area below the ladder did the trick. That gave birth to the fear of walking beneath ladders. Because a person never knew. The spirit or spirits of highwaymen or cutthroats might still haunt the space where they'd been executed.

Spirits of the evil crowded the Earth to avoid their destiny in Hell. The dead suffered no hangovers, she hoped.

As she watched the paramedics, she took an Ativan and chased it with an Ambien. She had a headache. She often had a headache, but maybe she'd forget this was her head. Ambien could do that. Enough Ambien.

In light of the circumstances, someone ought to offer a prayer. "Our Father who art in heaven," she began, but the Ambien was already erasing her thoughts. She started and stopped, at a loss for the right words. "Forget us our trespasses," she said, "as we forget those who've trespassed against us…"

Seventeen floors below her window, the paramedics had loaded their passenger and were slamming the doors. In the building across the way the single light winked out.

In its place, replacing the dad-shaped man, Mitzi saw only her own reflected outline. She waved an arm and watched her mirrored self waving back.

Her phone chimed. The ambulance was gone.

Alone, alone and beyond her reach, her mirrored self lifted an arm and put her mirrored phone to her ear. With her free hand, the reflection in the window waved. As if she were waving good-bye to the paramedics or to the dead person or just waving farewell to her real self.

From Oscarpocalypse Now *by Blush Gentry (p.1)*

Don't call me a movie star. I'm not, not anymore. I'm a certified gemologist these days. If I'm offered roles, it's not for my acting acumen. The last parts I want to play are the sort of freak show cameos that Patty Hearst got duped into.

No, what really excites me is chromium diopside. My company has controlling interest over the largest deposit of chromium diopside in Siberia. *More Emerald than Emeralds*, that's our slogan. What we mean is chromium diopside is a deeper green than most emeralds. My entire line is showcased on the *Blush Gentry Hollywood Crown Jewels Hour* on GemStoneTV.

My son, his name is Lawton, he's eleven. My husband, he's still in the industry but not in front of the camera. He works in postproduction, *post*-postproduction, like *deep postproduction*. And he's a little bit of a workaholic. He tells me, "Blush, my work is my church."

And, no. We didn't know anything about any grisly killings, at least not at the time they were being committed.

Whatever magic Robb worked, it got Foster sprung. From the airport he drove Foster to a diner. They took a booth near a woman wearing oversized sunglasses who pushed a package across her table toward a man who pushed it back. Anonymous behind her dark lenses, the woman fiddled with her phone. She clicked a pen and jotted something into a notebook.

The waitress hadn't brought out their eggs before Robb covered his face with both hands and burst into tears. "It's Mai," he sobbed, his words muffled behind his fingers. "It's everything." Customers turned to stare.

His wife, Mai, had left him after their baby's awful death. Foster had heard the story often enough at the support group.

Robb opened his jacket to reveal a shoulder holster, a gun snugged flat against his ribs. He wiped his face with a paper napkin. His other hand fumbled a buckle and snaps until the holster came loose, and he placed it and the gun on the table between them. "I can't have it right now. I can't say what will happen if I walk out of here with this..." He pushed it toward Foster.

Foster slid the gun back. Heavy steel against laminated plastic, the sliding sounded big. Like static. Like something grinding in a room where everyone present had gone silent.

They were two men sitting in a diner. One man crying, a gun resting between them, people stared. The woman wearing sunglasses stared.

"Please," Robb begged. "Just for now, you take it."

After the airport, Foster owed the man a favor. So Foster took the gun.

Mitzi arrived at the diner. The booth near the back. The usual arrangement. A producer, Schlo, sat waiting. With two projects backlogged, it wasn't as if she needed the work. But Schlo was like family. Besides, this being Hollywood, who didn't want to play the hero? Mitzi slipped into the booth and asked, "You already tried Industrial Light and Magic?"

The guy didn't answer, not right away. That was Schlo all over. The speech pattern of someone who lived on his mobile phone. A man who left a wide margin around each statement to allow for the satellite delay. He said, "Industrial Light and Magic's not you."

Even in person, sitting across the table, Schlo was loud. Like he spent his life yelling at the hands-free phone in his car.

Big Schlo lifted a hand to stroke the stubble on his cheek, clearly watching his reflection in her sunglasses. They gave her away, sunglasses, indoors. "Hang one on, last night?" he asked. "Xanax bars." He leveled a thick finger at her. His wrist sparkled with a ruby cuff link. "I'm maybe going to send you over some."

That, that she wouldn't dignify with a response.

"If it's magnesium you're not getting, Brazil nuts are your answer." He cupped a hand next to his mouth and whispered, "You know, back in my day we used to call them 'African American Toes'?" He hissed wetly, snickering at his own joke.

Mitzi lifted her glasses to glower at him, but the fluorescent lights stabbed her eyes.

He reached a hairy, meaty hand across the table. "You take after your mother. Such a person of goodness she was." His fingertips stroked her cheek. "You're not your father, you aren't. A bigger prick I never met than your father."

She slapped the hand away. The headache drove down her neck, across her shoulders and onward down her spine.

She'd only suggested Industrial Light & Magic to make a point. She was baiting the guy. Only Mitzi was Mitzi. She dodged eye contact. Signaled a waitress. Said, "Call Jenkins, she's good."

After the pause, Schlo said, "Jenkins won't touch this one." Again, too loud.

Mitzi set her phone on the table. She uncoiled a pair of earbuds and plugged them into the phone, saying, "I want you should hear a new scream."

Big Schlo waved off the pitch. To him a scream was a scream.

People, Mitzi asked herself, what do they know? They think they know the sound of a bone breaking, when all they know is celery. Frozen celery wrapped in chamois and snapped in half. How they think a skull sounds when someone jumps off a skyscraper and slams headfirst on the sidewalk, that's just a double layer of soda crackers glued to a watermelon and smacked with a baseball bat.

Your average moviegoer thought all knives made the same noise going in. The poor innocents wouldn't know the true sound of arterial spray until it was their own head-on car accident.

Schlo lifted a thick express-mail packet from the seat next to him. Handed it across the table. A sticky shadow of glue showed where an address label had been peeled off.

Mitzi lifted the flap. Her thumb riffed the stack of bills on top. All hundreds. Stacks and stacks. The scene in question must really stink.

Something popped. Gum popped. A gum-chewing server had stepped to their table. An orange-stained Los Angelina she wasn't. Not yet another bimbo beat hard with the blonde stick.

The waitress looked at Schlo too long. Then looked away too fast. She'd pegged him. Her spine straightened. She pushed out her chest and raised her chin. Turned her head in both directions for no reason except perhaps to display each profile. She asked, "What can I get you guys?" No longer a waitress, now she was an actor playing a waitress. With a tiny gulp she swallowed her chewing gum.

She started into reciting the specials. Delivered each word like here was an audition.

Mitzi cut her off. "Just coffee." She added, "Please."

When the server was gone, Schlo tried a new strategy. Said, "I love your work." He said, "That picture in release last month, the one where the kid gets tripped at the top of the stairs and busts his noggin open on the stone floor...that was yours, right?"

A kid, some actor played a teenager stalked by a haunted doll. The doll was a computer model. The actor was almost middle-aged. What tumbled down the flight of stairs was a lifelike dummy with an articulated skeleton inside. What made all this make-believe garbage real was the sound. The smack of somebody's skull splitting open on a stone floor and the perfect squash of the brains inside. That sound was the money shot that sold the scene.

Mitzi said, "A head of lettuce, frozen, and dropped to land next to the mic."

Schlo shook his oversized noggin. "This town knows a head of lettuce when they hear one." Insiders knew plywood strips soaked in water to dissolve the glue, then dried in the sun and snapped in half to dub a shattered femur.

Mitzi shrugged. On her phone she cued up the audio file she was shopping around. Her latest scream, it was the future of motion pictures. Acting beyond acting.

It was a shitty double standard. Visually, pictures were better every year. With computer graphics. With digitally animated everything. But sound-wise, it was still two coconut shells for every shot showing a horse. It was somebody mashing a bag of cornmeal for every step an actor took in the snow. The delivery was better, with Dolby and Surround and layered tracks, but the raw craft was still the fucking Middle Ages.

Thunder was a sheet of metal. Bat wings were an umbrella opened and closed at the appropriate speed.

"What's your scene?" Mitzi asked. She'd find out soon enough from the clip, but there were basic questions she needed answered up front.

Schlo looked away. Looked out the big windows at a Porsche parked in the lot. He said, "Nothing special. A young lady gets herself stabbed."

Mitzi plucked a little spiral notebook from her handbag. She clicked a ballpoint. "The make of the knife?"

Schlo frowned. "You need that?"

Mitzi started to slide the envelope of money across the table to where it came from.

Schlo slid it back. He held up a finger for patience while he fished out his phone and scrolled through something on the screen. Reading, he said, "A German Lauffer Carvingware. Stainless steel with an ebony handle. A seventeen-inch slicing knife, manufactured in 1954." He looked up. "You need a serial number?"

The waitress reentered the scene. She'd pinned her hair back, off her face. Her lipstick looked fresh and glossy. Her lashes sagged, long and fat with added mascara. Smiling as if this were a second callback, she held a couple

THE INVENTION OF SOUND

cups in one hand. A pot of coffee in the other. In a single take she placed the cups on the table and poured them full. She exited.

Mitzi jotted notes. "The knife stay in, or is this a multiple?"

Schlo looked up from his phone. "What's it matter?"

Mitzi shoved the fat packet of money back across the table. She clicked her pen and feigned putting away her notebook.

She didn't say as much, but with a multiple there would be the sound of the knife coming out. A suction noise. A sucking followed by the rush of blood or air from inside the wound. It was complicated.

As Schlo pushed the money back, he said, "Three stabs. One, two, three, and the knife gets left inside."

Without looking up from her note-taking, Mitzi asked, "Where's she stabbed?"

The producer eyed the pen, the notebook. He picked up his cup and slurped. "In a big brass bed."

Exasperated, Mitzi sighed heavily. "Where on…her… body?"

Schlo looked around. His color rose, and his eyes narrowed as he leaned across the table. He whispered something to her from behind his raised hand.

Mitzi shut her eyes and shook her head. She opened them.

His eyes narrowed to slits, the producer glowered. "Don't get all high-and-mighty with me." He smirked.

A sneer showed bottom teeth capped and bleached but no less ugly. "You did that scene where the demon dogs ripped the skin off that faggot priest." He was sputtering, juiced with equal parts shame and outrage. The few other diners looked up and glanced their way.

She didn't invent any of these scenarios, but Mitzi didn't say as much. She was just a woman, an independent contractor, making some writer's twisted dream come true.

Across the way a man seated at a table began to weep. Cupped both hands over his face, he did, and let loose loud, stagy sobs. A second man seated across from the first glanced around, his face going brick red with shame. This second man, just some dad-shaped nobody, he was, but his face Mitzi knew.

Back at his office, small girls continued to haunt Foster. Third graders ran photocopies. Middle schoolers pushed the mail cart, but he kept his monitor angled so they couldn't see. Their whispers and giggles drifted to him from the hallway and the offices beyond, but he stayed on task. In his leather swivel chair, he pretended to sip a cup of coffee. Sales reports lay open across his desk. One hand he kept always ready, one fingertip always resting on the key that would toggle him to a screen filled with part numbers and delivery dates.

The workaday world eddied around him as he snaked his way through secret online portals. Typing passwords.

Directed to links embedded in emails sent to him in exchange for a credit card number or crypto currency. Using a list of usernames, he hit sites that redirected him to sites that redirected him to JPEG bins where no one's IP address could be traced. There, Foster clicked through images people refuse to believe exist.

A coworker from the Contracts department stuck her head in the doorway. "Gates, you have a second?" she asked. "I'd like you to meet my daughter, Gena." A younger version of the woman, a girl standing elbow-high to her, stepped into view.

His red-rimmed eyes looked her way, he smiled. The very picture of a harried district rep, he said, "Hello, Gena."

The girl carried a manila folder. Pages and slips of paper dangled and fluttered from the edges of the folder. She looked at him with solemn eyes, her gaze taking in his office. "Where's your little girl?"

Her mother petted the child's hair. "Sorry, she thinks everyone should have a daughter she can play with."

A few degrees beyond the woman's field of vision, atrocities were worming across Foster's monitor. Playing in lurid color, the sound muted, here were crimes against children just the witnessing of which would send him to prison until he was an old, old man. With just one more step, she'd see things that would trouble her sleep for the rest of her life. Men wearing masks and waiting in line. Sex where the child was clearly dead.

Foster tapped a key, and the horrors were replaced by columns of serial numbers. He said, "Gena?"

The girl looked back, her eyes confused.

He continued, "You have a good 'Take Your Daughter to Work Day,' okay?"

Gena stepped closer. Her head tilting to a slight angle as she asked, "Why are you crying?"

He touched the side of his face and found a tear he wiped with his knuckles. "Allergies," he told her.

Her mother mouthed the words, "It's Tuesday." Stretching them out. She put a hand on her child's shoulder and steered her away.

Right. Taco Tuesday. Only in prisons and aboard submarines were people more excited about food than they were in office jobs. It was lunchtime, and the floor was going quiet. Foster toggled back to hell.

To find these sites had been spooky-easy. One anonymous phishing email had led him down the rabbit hole. Each cache yielded links to others.

So what if someone caught him? Who really cared if somebody from IT found anything he'd failed to scrub from his browser history? Foster risked nothing. He'd become a man who'd already suffered the worst. This searching gave him a reason to live.

Robb had told him, once, in the group, that the laboratories that did medical experiments and product testing on animals sought out dogs and cats that had once been household pets. Wild animals or strays living on the street knew how dangerous the world actually was. Such animals had a survival instinct, and they fought back. But animals raised with love would tolerate torture and regular abuse and never strike out in self-defense. On the contrary, animals raised in loving homes would suffer the laboratory abuse and always strive to please their tormenter. The more torture an animal could endure, the longer it was useful. And the longer it would live.

The same went for kids. Girls like his daughter, Lucinda, they could stay alive by not resisting. No child had been raised with more love than Lucinda, if she was still alive.

If nothing else, he might see how his daughter had died. Hovering over the images, reflected dimly on the screen was his dull, sick face. His eyelids sagging, half closed. His lips hanging half open.

Foster's eyes tried to avoid the kids the way anyone decent looked away from a dead cat in the street. To not look was to respect its dignity, somehow. These kids, they'd been looked at to death. Drooled over to death. And whatever took place in these images amounted to a slow-motion murder.

No, the kids Foster tuned out. The kids he found online with men. The men, though, he studied their faces. The pixilated ones, he studied their hands, or he scoured their bodies for tattoos, for finger rings or scars. An occasional glimpse of Lucinda's long hair might catch his attention— hair like that of the girl at the airport—but it was never her. So he focused on the men.

These kids, he'd never see them on the street. Foster knew as much. His only hope was to see one of the men. So he toggled to make screen captures, and he enlarged them as much as their resolution would allow. In that way he built his inventory of male faces, of tattoos and birthmarks. In such numbers it was just a matter of time. If he could catch just one man, he might be able to torture his way to the next.

Gates Foster saw himself as a bomb primed to explode. A machine gun in constant search of its next target. This, this office, no it wasn't his dream job. His fantasy career would be to torture these men who tortured children.

Crazy risks Mitzi didn't take.

A gun on the table across the restaurant from her. Two strange men, two goons trading a gun with one man crying and the other looking around for eyewitnesses. She let her gaze drift out the large windows to where a Porsche sat. Guarded, she lowered her voice. "I want you should give this a listen…" She offered Schlo the earbuds attached to her phone. When she dared to look again, the two men were gone.

The producer continued, wary. "The girl we hired, she's okay at taking off her clothes, but she couldn't scream her way out of a paper bag."

Cued up on her phone was Mitzi's new masterpiece. A game changer that would have sound replacing visuals as the most important part of any picture.

Schlo eyed the earbuds. "What's this?" He reached to accept them. He pressed one, then the other, into his hairy ears.

Mitzi winked. She said, "Judge for yourself." Touched the screen of her phone.

She didn't say as much, but the only way a person had to process an experience so troubling was by sharing it. And not just pirated on a telephone screen. A troubled person wanted everyone else to see and hear it on the big screen. Multiple times. Ticket after ticket. Until the experience stopped leaving them so shaken.

Over the phone, her masterpiece worked its magic. Schlo's face had gone pale as a powdered doughnut. A tear tipped out of each eye and slid down. His lower lip trembled, and he planted both hands over his mouth and looked away.

She spoke wistfully. "I call it *Gypsy Joker, Long Blonde Hair, Twenty-Seven Years Old, Tortured to Death, Heat Gun.*" She lifted her sunglasses, but only for a wink. "Catchy title, don't you think?"

Schlo plucked out an earbud. Bumped his cup and sloshed coffee. Snatched a napkin from the dispenser and mopped the table. He ripped out the other earbud and flung them both at her. Pushing himself away from the table, he shoved, red faced, past the waitress. As his parting shot, he muttered, "You should maybe see a priest."

Mitzi gathered the fallen earbuds, calling after him, "My work is its own church."

The server watched him exit through the glass doors and stagger across the parking lot toward his Porsche. She said, "I love his films." A waitress playing an actress playing a waitress.

Mitzi looked her up and down. She nodded after the Porsche. "You want to be in his next release?"

The girl asked, "You a producer?" She looked to be twenty-three, twenty-four, with just a trace of corn-fed twang to her words. She hadn't been in the Southland long enough to fry her skin and hair. No wedding ring, either. Promising details.

Mitzi looked at her nametag. "Shania? You know what a Foley artist is?"

She shook her head, Nuh-uh. "But you know people, right?"

In response Mitzi lifted the packet from the table and fished out a thick bundle of bills. She thumbed off one, two, three hundred and held them up, waiting to see whether or not this new talent would take the bait.

Robb called him at home. To check in, he said. He asked if Foster would be at the group for their next meet-up.

Foster studied the bite mark on his hand. The small horseshoe of baby teeth, scabbed over in fresh blood. And he told Robb to look for him in the church basement.

Before he could hang up, Robb's voice barked something, words pent up until this last chance. Foster brought the phone back to his ear and waited for a repeat.

Robb asked, "Why Denver?"

Foster fished his memory for how long he'd known Robb. When they'd met in the group, any details Robb had shared about Robb's own dead child, an infant, a son, back when Foster had first joined the support group.

Again, Robb asked, "What's so important in Denver?"

Foster bit back the truth. A monster was in Denver. A chat room avatar had let slip that Paolo Lassiter would be doing a piece of business there. Nobody was anyone on the dark web, but this chat room stranger had called Lassiter a big name in child sex trafficking, and said he'd be stopping over in Colorado for a day, maybe two.

Denver had been a long shot. But Foster had loaded his phone with screen grabs of Lassiter and made a list of the most likely hotels and set off on a fantasy of throttling the kingpin and beating out a confession about Lucinda.

If he told Robb that much, Foster would be needled to confess about his entire descent into chat rooms and galleries, and that would negate all his good intentions.

Instead, Foster said, "I was meeting a girl." He paused as if he were embarrassed, but actually to cobble together more lies. "I met a girl online. We might, you know, get married."

By now his luggage would be touching down in Denver. Going around the baggage claim carousel. Maybe even in transit back to him.

The line went quiet. Foster listened for sounds in the background, hints of Robb's life since his son's death. There was nothing. His wife had walked out. Robb might've been calling from a government bunker, the silence was so thick.

"Don't lie to us," said Robb, his voice burning with contempt. "You're not trying to resolve anything." Playing some ace, he added, "We know exactly who the girl in Denver is, and you ought to be ashamed of yourself." And as if to drive home the shame, he lowered his voice and said, "The entire group knows!"

It was Foster's turn to be stumped and confused, confused and frustrated, frustrated and to hang up the phone.

The past lived on in her hands, the way they'd shaken when Mitzi took her first DAT into a pitch. The memory lived as pain in her scalp, the old tug of her hair. She'd such long hair back then. High school–long hair, she'd pulled it tight, knotting it into a French braid she'd pinned down. Her French braid pinned to the back of her head, pinned as cruelly as any butterfly or scarab beetle pinned to the board in freshman-year Biology of Insects.

Mitzi Ives, schoolgirl Mitzi, she'd suffered the pins as both the board and the bug to be stared at.

Her hairstyle she winced to recall, the way it showcased her neck. The way her neck skin had glowed red when the producer eyeballed her chest and rubbed a hand over the blue stubble of his cheeks and chin.

The way her shoulders curved inward. How Mitzi hunched forward and crossed her arms. Her entire body was a recording of that first sales pitch.

"Miss Ives," said the producer, not Schlo. He looked at something written on his blotter. "Mitzi."

He wasn't Schlo. She'd worried Schlo would recognize the scream. Her career would begin and end with that sit-down. A rival of Schlo's this had been. He'd nodded for her to take a seat opposite his desk, then he'd sat. Perched he had, on the front edge of his desk, perching himself in her face, so close she could smell the starch in his shirt.

She'd skipped school half a day. Ditched a quiz in Popular American Politics, and missed a session in the language lab and a lecture on Intro to Fractals.

She'd worn her school uniform on the bus, her pleated, plaid tweed skirt. The blouse with capped sleeves and a Peter Pan collar with the top two buttons undone. Her feet remembered the shoes, too-big high heels left behind after her mother had taken a powder.

The chair she sat in was stylishly low, its seat wasn't a fart off the floor. Low, precisely so her skirt would slip toward her waist. Low so that she'd be forced to lean forward to tug the hem of the skirt and clamp it between her knees. At the same time, bending forward, her collar dipped to where not-Schlo could peer down the front of her blouse. Ordinary clothes. In her bedroom such clothes had been a uniform. Professional Frumpy. Here they felt like a music video striptease. Around her, the usual Berber rugs and chrome lamps. A wall of windows framed a view of Netflix.

At her eye level had been his crotch. Handshake distance.

Here was a tricky moment. In this game she'd never played, Mitzi had brought a tape player loaded with the DAT and cued up. She'd sweetened and fattened the scream, listened and relistened until she'd no idea whether it was any good or not. The player she'd set on the floor at her feet. Her feet still felt the wadded toilet paper she'd crammed into the toes of her too-big high heels.

Not-Schlo, his necktie a pointer, a striped silk arrow, red silk, it pointed down from his face to his crotch. This her eyes couldn't forget: How he could perch there and look at any point on her face and body. Stare up her skirt. Down her blouse. While she couldn't look at the one stuffed, crammed-full bulge, the swelling that eclipsed his belt buckle. Like a miniature belly it looked, stuffed like her shoes were stuffed. Between the belly-belly hanging down and that bulge rising up, his belt buckle was almost lost. None of this could she look at.

That was his power.

She brought the tape player to her lap. Like armor she wore it. Like a blocky, heavy, high-tech fig leaf, its speaker was positioned as if the sound would come wailing out of her.

Not-Schlo, he grunted. "What have you brought to

interest me, young lady?" His hand went to his mouth and wiped his lips. His throat shifted up and down as he swallowed, hard, making the knot of his tie bob. A shining red-silk Adam's apple.

Mitzi fumbled the buttons on the player. Tape squealed at high speed past the head. She clicked Rewind and brought the numbers on the counter back. The next appointment waited beyond the door. Voices were already trespassing to pull the focus off of her moment.

Mitzi felt weak. She'd failed. She would always fail.

Her body continued to be the black box of a jetliner that had crashed with no survivors.

She pressed Play.

A hiss of room tone followed. Then, her art.

Not just her hands or her neck but her entire body felt the rush. She was more than her body and mind. When the scream played, she felt plugged into the eternal, as if she were channeling something from the next world. She'd created something immortal, worth more than money, a thing no bean counter could create.

This was her power.

The scream rang out, and the shift occurred. The reversal. Now the producer was reduced to being merely a body. His mouth gaped to mimic the sound. That was the hallmark of the best gesture or catchphrase. Like a fishhook, it sank barbs into the audience and became part of them. A parasite, this scream was. The not-Schlo's eyes bugged even as his belly and crotch shrank away. They bugged and clamped shut as if suffering the same pain her actor had felt. The producer's mouth yawned, dropping his chin into his neck, and the all of him reared back as if Mitzi had shot or stabbed him. As if she a prizefighter was, and she'd pasted him a roundhouse punch to his glass jaw.

After the tape returned to its dull hiss, the room continued to vibrate. The voices from the waiting room had fallen to silence. Silence until the small words of one distant stranger asked, "What the fuck was *that*?"

In the office, the producer looked around. The bookshelves weren't the shelves they'd been. The framed photographs had become something strange. Every pen and book had shifted to become an animal menace in this confusing jungle, and a new host of chemicals appeared to surge through his body, the tears welling in his eyes, the flushed, forked veins that rose out of his buttoned-down collar.

Such a rush Mitzi had felt recording that first scream.

Everyone wanted to have an effect. People spent their lives trying to get a laugh. Or to seduce an audience of strangers. The goal was to commodify something, repeat it, sell them, these the most intimate of human drives. It meant turning people's basic humanity into something that could be bought and sold. From fast food to porn, this was power.

The producer shook his head until his cheeks flapped. He lurched to his feet and staggered behind his desk to slump into his chair. Even the swivel chair, black leather and button tufted, made a squeak like a beast, like a throat cut, and not-Schlo lifted his hands from the arms of the chair and recoiled into a small ball balanced there.

Mitzi's body never forgot that feeling. To vault from being a nobody to being the most important person in the room. Prey to predator.

She moved her hand as if to press Play once more, and the producer waved to stop her.

"Don't," he begged her. "My heart."

That, the shift from frightened to frightening.

Before that day, any rude bus driver could make Mitzi cry. Henceforth, her career would be to make everyone else cry. She'd jumped rank to become a professional bully, but better. This was tantric, the way she'd create universal tension, then trigger a united blast of relief. It was sexual, a smidgen more than almost.

Still two years shy of graduation, and she'd never gone back to class. After that day, the high school had sent truancy letters to her father. But from that point she'd been the only Ives in Ives Foley Arts.

Fractals would be for other fifteen-year-old girls to conquer. College-track girls. Mitzi knew all there was to know about life and violent death and cutting deals with back-end points allotted against the international net box office. Mitzi knew what tortures would spoil a scream.

The voices in the outer office remained silent. Now they were listening to her. The producer, not-Schlo, he reached a spotted hand inside his suit coat and brought out a rattling bottle of pills. One of these he tipped into his palm and tossed onto his tongue.

For a while Mitzi had called her work "politics." To her mind, women had never been allowed to kill. Not unless they were threatened. Women could never kill for the sheer pleasure, and they could never kill another woman. Despite all the fuss about universal child care and income inequality, killing was the real measure of a woman's progress. As the thrill of that first recording session had ebbed, Mitzi told herself that collecting screams amounted to a political act. It constituted the ultimate power.

To her mind, it amounted to Last Wave Feminism.

Eventually, her motives would evolve. As she continued to chase that first high, Mitzi would come to think of the work as a gift. In classic displacement, she tried to find her joy in others. She was redeeming the anonymous lives of anonymous people, giving them an immortality they'd never dared imagine. Mitzi Ives: Star Maker.

But each new motive was just a step further from the truth. It wasn't political or benevolent, what Mitzi did she did for power. The ever-diminishing marginal rewards of that first brush with power.

She'd never taken a drink or a pill. Those would come soon, when the stories she told herself had begun to wear thin.

The producer, not-Schlo, he'd gathered his wits. His

eyes counted numbers Mitzi couldn't see, and he said, "I'll give you twenty thousand for exclusive world rights."

Mitzi set the DAT player at her feet and crossed her legs. She let her skirt ride up. To see if he'd look, to see if the power had truly shifted to her.

He didn't look. "Okay, twenty-five," he'd said.

"Thirty," Mitzi countered. She leaned forward and allowed her neckline to dip low. To display the almost-legal shape of her breasts.

He continued to not look. She'd proved herself to be someone *that* dangerous.

A sneer, not a real sneer, more a reflex he'd used on too many pitches in the past, it pulled his mouth to one side. "Nobody's paid that much for a scream." He said, "Crazy to think—"

Mitzi stood and smoothed her skirt. "You want to try for forty thousand?" She made as if to take her things and leave.

He snapped. Fear would sell him, the dread that a rival would spend the forty grand and leverage the scream to make a fortune. Such a scream, it could be licensed and sub-licensed to films and television, to video games. Telephone ring tones. Greeting cards! Screams needed no translation to reach foreign markets. The trickle down would never end. It would be a profit engine forever.

"Sit, sit, sit!" he'd said and patted the air as if he could shove her back into that low-low chair. He rummaged through a desk drawer and dug out a checkbook. If he balked, she'd take the recording wide. By next week not-Schlo would be bidding against an army of sound engineers and special effects gurus. Testing a pen, he asked, "What do you call this…masterpiece of yours?"

The question gave Mitzi pause. It was like naming a first child, something so important she'd neglected to give it any thought. According to her watch, the meeting had gone beyond its allotted time. Other pitches would be piling up in the outer office, all those strangers listening. They'd hate her for hogging so much time.

She found she enjoyed being hated.

Here was her brilliant new career: to attract the listening of a billion strangers.

"I call it…," she said and waited. Timing was everything. "Serial Killer Flayed to Death by Child." She added, "And let's round the price up to a hundred thousand dollars, shall we?"

The producer didn't respond.

The faint sound of his scratching, his pen scratching her name and the number one hundred thousand on a check, that sound would echo forever, recorded in her ears.

No one spoke at first. The group of them sat around the basement, casting looks at each other. A former mother looked at a former father who looked at the group leader. No one looked at Foster. Then they were all looking at the group leader, Robb. Robb looked at Foster and asked, "So, how's Bali?"

Foster looked down at his hands, at his hands in his lap.

A doctor whose son had gone bicycle riding and forgotten to wear his helmet, just once, just that one time, just a quiet ride around the neighborhood is all it was, a story Foster had heard him recount until Foster could tell it himself, this man took a phone from his coat pocket. The doctor brought up a web page and held it for the group to see. He said, "I understood your daughter was dead?"

People craned their necks to look. Others brought up the same page on their own phones. One member said, "So she's not dead, your Lucinda?"

His brow wrinkled with confusion, another member studied his phone. "A dead girl this most certainly is not."

The group leader, Robb, held up his hand for silence. To Foster, he said, "I was afraid of something like this." The picture of empathy, he urged, "Tell us, again, how Lucinda died." After a beat, he added, "Please."

There was nothing Foster hadn't already told. She'd stepped into an elevator.

The group, this group amounted to a kind of addiction treatment. To Foster, they were all recovering from their love for a dead child, and they wanted him to follow the same path, but he couldn't. He wouldn't abandon his addiction. And maybe they envied him his denial. Each of them had seen his or her son or daughter removed from life. They'd identified the remains. Held a funeral. Only he had the option to pretend his child still existed, somewhere.

The woman in the photos they perused, she had Lucinda's fall of wavy auburn hair. College age or thereabouts. The woman smiling beside him at the rail of a cruise ship, her eyes and mouth were the adult version of the eyes and mouth of the second grader smiling beside a much younger Foster in other photos.

Yes, his child, yes, Lucinda, yes, she was dead. This other Lucinda, so beautiful and still alive on her social media page, she was a coping mechanism. Why bother explaining? His reasons would never sink in.

Another member of the group held up a video clip of this full-grown Lucinda and Foster, her father, in the basket of a hot-air balloon. Far below them acres of grapevines flowed in parallel straight lines across a landscape of low hills. This member asked, "Gaslighting us, maybe?"

Another corrected. "'Trolling' the young people call it nowadays."

The group leader continued to press. "If...If she's really been missing over seven years, you need to finally file with the medical examiner for a Presumption of Death Order."

How could Foster make them see? It wasn't how it looked. He flexed his hand, balling his fingers into a fist and then spreading them wide. Letting the pain from the airport bite mark distract him.

Robb shushed the group. "Friend," he asked. "Is your child dead or alive?"

Foster began the story he always told. "We'd gone to my office. Lucinda stepped into an elevator—"

Robb interrupted. "Then you need to hold a funeral." He meant an empty-casket ceremony, a memorial service where all her false friends and distant social media followers could pay their last respects to a coffin filled with her old dolls and stuffed animals and clothes. Pallbearers would carry this to an open grave. In short: a hollow ritual.

As the harangue continued, his phone buzzed. A text appeared on the screen. From Lucinda.

This Lucinda, alive and beautiful and so addictive, she asked: Up for next week?

The girl on the bed stirred. She blinked slowly, and her lips curved into a loopy, dopey smile. Her bare arms and legs twisted, stretching against the rope that held her wrists and ankles tied to the posts of the rented brass bed. Her movements crinkled the clear-plastic sheeting that protected the mattress. It had taken Mitzi longer than she'd expected to assemble the bed, an antique delivered from a properties warehouse. She'd hardly had time to position the monitor and move the mic booms into roughly the right locations before the Rohypnol had started to wear off.

She lowered a Shure Vocal SM57 until it almost touched the girl's lips. Next to it, an old-school ribbon mic waited, like something left over from Orson Welles's radio days. Reaching in from other directions were can mics. A shotgun mic dangled down. Each connected to its own preamp.

She waited for the girl to speak, watching for the needles to jump on each of the VU meters in this, her palace of analog.

The needles twitched as the girl spoke. "Oh, it's you." She gave Mitzi a slow-motion, underwater wink. Lifting her chin, she looked down at her exposed breasts, her complete nakedness.

Mitzi nudged a mic closer. "You fell asleep during our talk."

The girl sighed with relief. "I was afraid this was a rape."

In response to a monitor, Mitzi withdrew a mic a smidgen. She said, "I need to check my levels. Can you tell me what you had for breakfast?"

Still woozy from the sedative, the girl lifted her face toward the Shure. So close she looked at it cross-eyed, she began, "Pancakes. Potatoes. French toast." Clearly playing along, inventing things, she continued, "Scrambled eggs, oatmeal, bacon…"

A waitress reeling off breakfast specials.

The popping *p*'s and *b*'s pegged the analog needles into the red. Oversaturating the recording, making it warm. But clipping the digital, turning it into useless static. Mitzi pulled the Shure back a little more. She brushed a strand of pale hair off the girl's forehead, and doing so gently pressed the girl's head back down into the plastic-covered pillow.

Without resisting, the girl continued, "Orange juice, grapefruit juice, oatmeal…" Her eyes drifted shut as if she might once more fall asleep. Her restaurant uniform lay draped across the chair near the wall. Her stomach growled, making the needles jump. "Sorry," the girl mumbled. "All this food talk makes me hungry."

Mitzi wondered if she needed to readjust for room tone. She said, "Not to worry. You won't be hungry much longer."

She went to the chair where the girl's things sat and opened the purse. Removed a billfold. Sought out a driver's license and studied it. "Shania?" She stepped back to the bedside, repeating louder, "Shania, honey?" She spied, in the billfold, the three one-hundred-dollar bills she'd offered as bait. Mitzi retrieved the bills, folded them, and slipped them into a pocket of her jeans.

The girl's eyes opened. Her brow furrowed as her focus darted from one mic to the next as if she'd forgotten them.

Mitzi pressed on. "Do you know what the Wilhelm scream is, dear?" The girl's eyes found her own.

The girl shook her head. The driver's license had been issued in Utah. Jack Mormon because there'd been no special underwear to find when Mitzi had cut away the waitress uniform.

"You've heard it," Mitzi prompted, "the Wilhelm scream." It was a man's scream first recorded in 1951 for a film titled *Distant Drums*. In one scene, soldiers wade through an alligator-infested swamp, hence the scream's formal title, *Man, Getting Bit by Alligator, and He*

Screamed. Since it was created, the Wilhelm scream has been used in more than four hundred features, as well as countless television projects and video games.

"The classic screams have such elegant names," Mitzi continued. "Like paintings." The second most famous scream, for example, is titled *Man, Gut-Wrenching Scream and Fall into Distance.* "Like a masterpiece of art." This scream's more common name is "the Howie scream" because it was used to dub Howie Long's 1996 performance in *Broken Arrow,* but the scream itself was recorded for a 1980 film called *The Ninth Configuration.*

The third most famous industry scream was *The Goofy Holler,* but the less said about that the better.

A chime sounded. Her phone, sitting on the mixing console, it chimed again.

From the bed, the girl said, "You have a call."

Mitzi lifted the phone and held it to show the photo of a man. "My boyfriend. Jimmy."

"He's cute," said the girl, squinting.

Mitzi considered the photograph of a shaggy-haired greaser wearing an oil-stained bandanna knotted around his head. "You're still delirious." She waited for the call to go to voicemail. "He wants to hook up." She lifted her chin and turned her head to display some fading purple bruises around her neck. Doing so, she watched the monitor. Watching and rewatching the short clip the production company had asked her to loop. The monitor positioned so the girl on the bed couldn't see it. Mitzi knew she was droning on, but she needed the girl to be fully awake. There'd be no chance for a second take.

She lifted a FedEx mailer and felt the surprising weight inside it. Something so long and thin yet so heavy, it had to be metal. The shape of it obscured by layers of Bubble Wrap.

Healthy as the girl looked, hers wasn't the body type casting agents kept on file. Her lips parted. As if praying, she continued to whisper, "English muffins...biscuits and gravy..."

Mitzi stretched a latex glove over one hand. Watching the meters pulse softly, she stretched on the second glove then began to bundle her hair under a cloth surgical cap.

Clear as the girl's skin was, it hid nothing. Her face and neck flushed red while her hands and feet faded to a blue-white. Her breathing grew shallow. Beads of sweat pebbled her chest and belly.

On the mixing console a bottle of pinot gris sweated in a chrome bucket of ice. A cloisonné saucer held a few pills. Always the same saucer enameled with pink poppies, those flowers of forgetfulness. Always Ambien in the strongest dose available. Mitzi poured a glass of wine and took a few sips with a pill.

She wondered if Jack Mormons prayed. If they had prayers to recite when they found themselves naked and tied spread eagle in an acoustically perfect recording studio.

The Ambien seemed to push the blood through her veins a bit faster. The typical side effect had started, the mania. Before conking out, people on Ambien reportedly binged on ice cream. They went on internet or cable-television shopping sprees. Engaged in marathon sex with strangers. Even committed murder. Murders for which they'd later be acquitted because they had no memory of the event.

That was crucial, to have no memory of the event.

She poured her glass full again. With latex fingers she lifted a second pill from the saucer and drank it down.

On the video monitor the actors dressed as Confederate soldiers attacked the actress in the bed, the scene looping over and over again.

Mitzi reached up and pulled the shotgun mic a skosh closer to the girl's mouth. At a keyboard she typed in the name of this new file. Using a felt-tipped pen, she wrote the same on an old-style DAT cartridge. She wrote: *Praying Girl, Stabbed Brutally, Rapid Exsanguination.* She asked, "Now, Shania, tell me what else you ate for breakfast, please."

Pain never brought about the best results. No, severe pain only triggered shock. A doomed catatonia, silence as the last refuge of a mortally wounded animal playing possum. Only dread and terror brought out a marketable recording. A masterpiece.

Her voice reduced to a whisper, hushed as if she were praying, the girl said, "Two fried eggs…an English muffin…"

Mitzi tore open a small plastic package containing two

foam rubber plugs. With latex fingers she twisted one until it would fit inside of her ear.

The girl stopped after "…orange juice." Her eyes intent on Mitzi, she asked, "Will this be noisy?"

Mitzi nodded, twisting the second earplug into a small, tight cylinder. It wasn't lost on her that this army of microphones would continue to record even as the sleeping pills short-circuited her own memory. She struggled to recall the girl's name and how they'd met.

Before Mitzi could insert the second earplug, the girl asked, "Would you do me a favor?" Maybe she was still high, or it could've been denial, but the girl said, "I hate loud noise. Can I have earplugs, too?"

The monitors, their needles bounced softly with the request.

Mitzi was tearing open the express package, about to remove and unwrap the knife. But she considered the request. There was no reason the poor girl should have to listen. Mitzi drained her glass of wine. Swallowed another Ambien. She tore open a new package of foam plugs and twisted each before inserting it into the girl's warm, soft ears.

The face, the girl's blushing, teary-eyed face, mouthed the words, "Thank you."

Mitzi answered, "You're very welcome," but neither woman could hear the other.

Only the huddled microphones heard, leaning in, ready to collect the sound of what would have to happen next.

* * *

Foster asked to be seated with his back to the door. So he could hear her before she came into sight. For that same reason he'd arrived early and chatted up the maître d. He'd drunk half his Scotch when a voice behind him said, "Hello."

A young woman said, "My name is Lucinda, and I'm meeting my father for lunch."

He didn't turn, but waited.

"He's very handsome. Very distinguished," the voice added.

A man's voice, the maître d's, said, "Right this way, please."

It was worth the wait when she came into sight. Her mother's auburn hair, Lucinda wore it down on her shoulders the way he liked it best. His own blue eyes looked back at him as he stood to greet her. She was wearing the dress he'd bought for her in Singapore. The one she'd modeled on Instagram. They kissed cheeks. To the maître d, Foster said, "Alphonse, you've met my daughter?"

The gentleman stood by, saying, "So charming a young lady," as Foster seated her.

For the maître d's benefit, he asked, "Lucy, do you remember the time you stepped on the bee?" He smiled at the memory.

She was a quick study. "Of course." Quick on the uptake, she asked, "How old was I?"

"You were four." Foster loved how she knew to echo,

never to ad-lib. If she wasn't an actress, she ought to be. She was so gifted at spontaneous role-playing.

The waiter arrived and took her order for a glass of wine. Foster asked for another Scotch. Keeping to their long-established script, he asked about her classes in college. She was on the dean's list, of course. She asked his advice about graduate school. Her hand ventured across the table, and he reached forward and squeezed it with his own. She said, "It's so good to see you!"

Foster winced in pain. The bite mark on his hand. She didn't ask.

Unseen, his fingers pressed the usual fee into her palm. Two hundred in cash, plus another couple hundred as a tip. Their agreed-upon rate for a one-hour lunch. It might seem expensive, the dinners, the trips together, but it was better therapy than he'd gotten from any psychiatrist. To simply look at her filled him with joy.

How many years had it been? He'd used the latest age progression of her from the side of a milk carton. He'd gone online and surfed escort sites until he'd found an exact match.

A silence fell over the dining room, and all heads turned. The restaurant lighting dimmed. A waiter had entered from the kitchen carrying a small, elaborately decorated cake on which several small candles burned. No one sang, it was far too elegant an establishment, but muted applause erupted as the waiter delivered the birthday cake to the beautiful young woman. Lucinda beamed appropriately.

She brought her fingertips to her lips as if to stifle a cry of joy.

"Happy birthday, my darling," Foster said. He reached under the table to where a shopping bag waited. He brought out a small box wrapped in pink foil and frothing with ribbons.

Ignoring her candles, she slipped the paper and ribbons from the box and opened it to reveal a gleaming double strand of natural pearls. She gasped. Everyone watching gasped.

"They were your mother's," Foster said regarding the pearls. "And your grandmother's."

Not acting, not for the moment, she looked at him with genuine affection. He knew the difference. In this moment he hated the mourning support group for putting a stop to this sweet fantasy. The necklace coiled in its box. A satin-lined box not unlike a casket.

He nodded toward the cake, saying, "Make a wish."

The pink-polished fingertips of one hand touched the pearls. She regarded the cake before whispering, "I want to be in the movies." And as she followed her instructions, the tiny flames winked out, and a ghost of bitter smoke wafted over him.

The next sunrise wasn't her enemy. The Muzak in the elevator wasn't torture. Minus a hangover, odors, people's colognes, even the faint stink of bleach on her own hands, didn't cramp her stomach and spin her mind dizzy with pain. Without sunglasses she could sit in the waiting room and read the trades. Even in the Southland, only a few doctors' coffee tables offered the *Hollywood Reporter* and *Variety*, but Dr. Adamah wasn't just any doctor.

She'd awoken with no memory except the dream of assembling a complex something made of brass. All curves and shining, polished curlicues, accented with porcelain knobs hand painted with pink roses. It wasn't an unpleasant dream. It was a bed, a masterpiece of an antique brass bed.

As she sat waiting for her name to be called and thumbing through *Entertainment Weekly*, her phone chimed. A new text from a private number said: Magnificent results. Per usual.

Her inbox showed one new file. An audio file labeled Praying Girl. Those words, those and the whiff of bleach on her fingers brought back a dream. Something butchered. Someone slaughtering a pig. Something she must've seen on the television as she'd drifted off to sleep. The squealing shrieks, ghastly, and blood everywhere. Her shoulders ached as if she'd spent the night chopping wood.

As she turned a page, her phone chimed again. A new text asked: Yur $1M holler still avail?

Before she could text a response, a voice asked, "Mitzi?" She looked to where a young woman sat behind a carved and white-lacquered desk. This woman, the receptionist, said, "Dr. Adamah will see you now."

As Mitzi gathered her things, a door opened and the bearded doctor met her with the usual warm smile. They crossed a hallway to the open door of an examination room. Inside, a paper-covered table sat opposite a stainless-steel sink and a bank of glass-fronted cabinets. The doctor nodded for her to take a seat on the table.

Dr. Adamah asked, "Feeling better?" He sat, leaning back against the lip of the sink. Eyed the fading bruises around Mitzi's neck. "How's Jimmy?"

He meant Mitzi's latest boyfriend. The reason she wanted a tubal ligation.

The doctor reached toward Mitzi and curled an index finger, prompting. "You have something to give me?"

Mitzi leaned over her purse. She picked out three one-hundred-dollar bills.

The doctor took the money and held the bills over the sink. He took a cigarette lighter from a pocket of his lab coat and sparked a flame. This he held under the money until it blazed, and the smoke drifted toward the ceiling. Dr. Adamah followed Mitzi's glance to a smoke detector and assured her, "It's disconnected."

The burnt smell suggested sweat and plastic, plastic and aluminum foil. A foul whiff brought tears to Mitzi's eyes. As smoke rose, the crumbling flakes of charred rag paper drifted down into the sink. The flames neared the doctor's fingers, and he let the burning remnants drop. What remained, it curled and blackened against the steel. Larger flakes broke into smaller. The flames along the final edges burned blue and died. A last puff of smoke dispersed in the hazy room.

Mitzi peered into the purse nestled on the table beside her hip. Inside coiled a roll of bills. Back at her condo a room held nothing but money.

Before doctors had become sawbones...Before psychologists had been headshrinkers, they'd all been seers. They'd been fortune-tellers, temple whores, shamans. As such they were trained to read the best tells people presented. Subtle aspects of body language, skin tone, scent. They could diagnose the unrecognized problem by asking evocative, probing questions. At least that was how Dr. Adamah explained his gift. Having attended medical school in Port-au-Prince, he had a skill set that went beyond physical diagnosis. To him everything was a ritual. Ritual was everything.

How long had she been consulting with him? Mitzi sifted through her memory. Schlo it was, Schlo or some other producer who'd referred her. Back when the rage that had fueled her first kill was spent, and she'd needed something more to do the next job.

Mitzi wasn't sold on the mumbo jumbo, but she had no idea how penicillin worked. She'd still take it if need be.

Leaning over the sink, the doctor examined the scorched ashes as if they were tea leaves in a cup. He asked, "Does the name Shania Howell mean anything to you?"

At the mention of the name, Mitzi pictured the waitress from the diner but nothing more.

"She's at peace," said the doctor. "And you are forgiven because your actions have delivered her to a place of bliss and fulfillment beyond any she'd known on Earth."

Ready for the next part of the ritual, Mitzi took a pad of paper and a pen from her handbag.

The doctor studied the ashes. "Her parents reside at 947 East Placer Drive in Ogden, Utah."

Mitzi jotted down the address and waited.

"They owe," the doctor announced, "approximately eighty-five thousand on their second mortgage and thirty-one thousand on their originating."

Mitzi made a note to send two hundred thousand in cash. Her money room at the condo was as packed as any hoarder's warren. Stockpiled were so many bales and cartons of banded five-hundred-dollar bills, a person could hardly venture a step within the door. She scratched out the first number and resolved to send an anonymous carton containing three hundred thousand.

The smoke shifted, swirled and eddied in the small room like so many ghosts. A bitter smell. Legions of lost souls crowding around them. Mitzi tried not to inhale.

At the sink the doctor turned on the taps and used his fingers to direct the water so that it washed the ashes toward the drain. He dried his hands with a paper towel and pulled on a pair of latex gloves. Next, he opened a drawer and produced a blank sheet of paper, an envelope, a pen.

Placing the paper on the countertop, he spoke as he wrote, "Dear Mummers and Paw-paw..." This voice wasn't his own. It twanged and drawled. Neither was the handwriting his. The letters looped in the style of a high school student.

Mitzi had witnessed this before, too often to keep track of. Automatic writing channeled from the spirit world.

"Don't try to find me," continued the doctor. As he filled the page, Dr. Adamah said, "I love you and me-maw so much." These same words looped and scurried across the page. "She may not know it, but little Braylene is carrying a child, and she must marry the boy. It's decreed." The florid handwriting paused.

The doctor turned over the sheet and continued on the reverse side. "I will greet all of you, very soon, and we will all share our love forever." Dr. Adamah signed the letter with the name Shania.

His latex-gloved hands folded the paper and slipped it into the envelope. He wet a fingertip in the sink and rubbed it along the glue strip to seal the letter inside.

Not that Mitzi could make sense of it all, but the words of the letter washed her with a warm comfort. They seemed to absolve her of sins that Mitzi had made sure she couldn't recall. She knew not to ask for details. She didn't want to know more.

The doctor plucked a tissue from a box and wrapped the tissue lightly around the letter before offering the wrapped envelope.

Mindful not to leave fingerprints, Mitzi accepted it.

* * *

At the tail end of evening rush hour, Foster pulled to the curb. In front of the Student Union building she stood clutching a thick textbook. She waved and shouted, "Dad! Over here!" If the book was real or a prop, it was a nice touch.

She leaned in the driver's-side window and gave him a peck on the cheek. She darted around the front of the car and climbed in the shotgun seat. Clicked her seat belt. Placed the book between them on the seat. She was wearing the birthday pearls.

Foster panicked at the idea that without her to recite his stories, he'd forget them. But maybe that was the goal all along.

As he checked his side mirror and signaled to pull out, he asked, "Do you remember the pony we rented?"

He wanted to start her on easy events. Like testing her in some obscure catechism. First, the pony episode. Then, the roasting pan lesson. The Gospel of Lucinda. He'd drilled her until she must've known Lucinda's childhood better than she knew her own. He reached the book next to his hip and flipped it open. A text on the Dramatic Arts. He lay the usual fee between the pages and closed it.

As if unaware, she looked away, observing the buildings they passed. The people who lined the sidewalks.

Perhaps she was buying time to think. But now, her eyes bright with confidence, Lucinda threw herself into the role. "The pony? Of course I remember, Dog Biscuit." The correct name of the pony. "My last day in second grade." The correct occasion. "I wore these brand-new Keds I didn't want to get dirty — "

"They were red," Foster interrupted.

"They were blue. Light blue." She was right.

He wasn't trying to trip her up. He'd muffed a detail of something precious, and it scared him to think she knew his child's life better than he did. He shifted the conversation to something more obscure. "Remember Halloween?"

She asked, "Which one?" Guarded. A student undergoing a pop quiz.

"Your first," Foster coached her as he sailed the car through traffic. "When you were four."

This Lucinda brought a hand to her mouth and bit her thumbnail. She closed her eyes in concentration. Insisted, "Don't tell me."

Foster urged her along. "You were a witch."

"No." She drew out the word, stalling. Triumphant, she cried, "I was an elf!"

Unnerved, Foster changed lanes abruptly. A horn honked behind them. "You were?" He was losing hold of his most valuable possessions, his memories.

This Lucinda chided, "I wore my pink footy pajamas and my pink tutu from ballet class, you remember." Now she was dictating his memories. This imposter had taken authorship of his past.

He couldn't argue. He didn't remember. For the first time, he turned the tables. "Now you choose a story."

She touched a fingertip to her smooth forehead.

"Remember...the Christmas when your brother played Santa Claus?"

He couldn't and felt a flash of anger. He'd given away his child's life to this stranger. She knew Lucinda's life backwards and forwards.

She wasn't being cruel. Only blushed as if embarrassed on his behalf. Timidly she asked, "You remember my guinea pig?"

He poked around in his memory the way a person feels for a light switch inside the doorway of a dark room. Foster brightened. "Ringo."

Concern clouded her face. "Rufus," she corrected. Right again. They drove in silence for a few blocks. Almost at their destination, she asked, "Where are we headed, Dad?"

On the lookout for a parking space, he told her, "Don't call me that." Suddenly he'd broken character. She'd learned the game too well, and he was losing this contest. It felt like a classic reversal: the parent becoming the child, the child lecturing the elder.

A space opened up and he pulled the car into it. She glanced at her phone, if only to check the time. This was going to be a long hour.

"Thank you," she said, her voice hushed. "For the pearls, I mean." She touched them as if afraid he might want them back.

He lifted her book from the seat. "You recognize this?" He nodded over the steering wheel to indicate an

58

office tower down the block. A building as bland as a tombstone.

She leaned forward to peer through the windshield. "It's the Parker-Morris Building," she said, "where Daddy— where you used to work."

He climbed out of the car, carrying the textbook as bait so she'd follow. Striding down the sidewalk, he shouted back over his shoulder, "Do you remember how you got lost that one time?"

She climbed out her side and scurried after him.

"Yes," he continued, outdistancing her, "your mother and I never thought we'd find you again."

Rushing to keep pace, this Lucinda chirped, "It was Daddy-Daughter Day at your office…"

Without slowing, he demanded, "And?"

Stumbling between other pedestrians, now uncertain, she answered, "I wanted to play a game? I wanted to play elevator tag."

They'd arrived at the doorway to the tower. She kept reaching toward the book he held. Because she was actually a drama student or because her money was inside it, Foster couldn't tell. "Lucinda?" he asked. "You want to play a game with Daddy?"

Jimmy she dated for his legs. He had long legs that made it easy to plant a foot against the back of her head. He'd rolled her facedown and yanked her naked hips into the air. Jimmy, he'd only needed to watch the video once. Jimmy with his gummy dreadlocks and pockmarked cheeks. His nose like something found pickled in a jar after a hundred years. The whole of his lanky, leathery nakedness like something excavated from a peat bog. He never asked about the bruises left over from the last one. Or the scars on her arms and back from the ones before that. Jimmy had just watched the video on her monitor at the Fontaine. For men porn was like a tutorial.

The tiny man on the screen rolled the tiny woman face-down. He pulled her butt up until she was on her knees, but kept her face pinned to the floor by planting one tiny foot on the back of her tiny head. His other foot remained on the floor, and he bent that knee, lowering himself to sodomize her. Not everyone could mimic the position, but Jimmy could.

Like someone learning to dance, he'd carefully rolled her over and placed his bare foot on the back of her head. They were on the floor. The bed was too wiggly. Mimicking the video, he'd spat on her upturned asshole. His aim, warm and dead center. This, already an improvement over the Gypsy Joker who'd chewed tobacco.

His balance wavering, he wedged the head of his erection against her. For a moment half his body weight was drilling into her as he bent his other leg to lower himself. The pressure of his foot drove down on the nape of her neck, drove Mitzi's mouth into the carpet. Muffling her words as she insisted, "Harder! Step harder!"

The wine in her stomach surged up her throat, but

she choked it back down. Wine burning with bile and sleeping pills. She tried to twist her head and get more foot-stomping pressure against her cervical vertebrae. An internal decapitation is what she was angling for. It's why she'd trekked down to Riverside and braved the death glares of local homegirls until she'd met Jimmy. Jimmy with his long legs and his toenail fungus shoved tight against her jaw. The one before, the Gypsy Joker, even with his swagger and his meth-fueled need to fuck, he hadn't the lower body strength. Weren't motorcycles supposed to build up thigh muscle? He might take a couple halfhearted stomps against the back of her head. She could kick the heavy bag at the gym harder. Beyond that, he'd slap her around and choke her until she blacked out, but she'd always awoke to find him snoring in her bed.

What more was there to say? The Gypsy Joker's skin was so pale and he'd so little body hair that his abundant tattoos made him look like someone's wedding china. She'd find handfuls of her hair ripped out. Her scalp ached. No matter how many times she'd sat him down and made him watch the video, he'd only managed to knock out one of her front teeth and give her a small anal fissure that bled like the bejeezus and took over a month to heal.

Jimmy grunted. The man in the video said, "Give me that hole" and slapped the woman's ass.

Jimmy said, "Gimme that hole, bitch" and slapped Mitzi's thigh.

They were, both of them, slick with sweat. And they'd

been drinking wine so chances looked good. With each withdraw of his erection he lifted his center of gravity too high and threatened to topple. His was basically a three-point stance, like a milking stool, and any slip might force all of his weight against the fragile top of her spine.

Something popped inside her head, a popping sound, and blood flooded her mouth. But instead of her backbone, her nose had broken against the floor. Crushed sideways against the carpet, the cartilage had snapped with a crunch not unlike a dried crab claw.

A perfect sound effect wasted. Her mind, again, wandering, she wondered, If a nose was broken in the forest and no one was there to record it and dub it into a film, did the nose really break?

Foster let her assume the worst. He waved her into an elevator car and said, "Go up. Go down. Switch elevators. But if I catch you, you're dead." He reached inside his jacket and slid the pistol from its shoulder holster. Robb's gun. It wasn't loaded.

Security was still a joke here. Then as now, no guard manned the desk. The bank of security monitors showed empty hallways in grainy black and white. On one screen, he saw himself holding the gun, balding, his eyes bulbous behind the thick lenses of his glasses, one veined hand holding the gun. No one watched him. Only he watched.

Let the police come arrest him. The police wouldn't come. This wasn't that kind of world, not anymore. Maybe it never had been.

The gun was necessary to terrorize her. If this Lucinda feared him, she'd never phone him in the future. She'd never reappear just to say hello and chat about old times. He couldn't beat his addiction to her. She had to be dead to him.

She looked at him, cocked her pretty head. Whether she was truly an excellent actor or she saw something ruthless in his face, she blinked back tears. She looked over his shoulder as if for help, then reached forward and pressed the button for a floor. Backed slowly against the rear of the car.

"Use your phone," he warned her, "pull a fire alarm. But stay in one spot too long, and I'll find you before the police do."

Foster did what he should've done so long ago. Instead of giving chase he waited.

Her doors slid shut and the car began to rise according to the floor indicator. There in the lobby, a panel of stainless steel showed vertical rows of red lights, each marking the location of a different elevator. The car she'd boarded stopped on the seventeenth floor. Another light stopped on the same floor, then proceeded down a few floors. Clearly she'd switched cars to evade him.

The small red lights traced her path of escape, bobbing and weaving, bursting from an elevator on one side of the building to dash into another elevator and ride down or up further. Then, to switch cars once again.

What he did today would keep her running away from him for the rest of her life.

Foster's guess was that she'd panic soon. She might call the police or her pimp, but she'd never linger in one place lest Foster find her. His gut was right. One elevator was plummeting, an express straight for a lobby escape.

Watching it fall, Foster remembered how he'd chased his daughter during her long-ago game. He'd catch sight of her only as she ducked squealing into a different car. He'd make a grab for her, but she'd be gone. It was fun, he'd thought. A game.

It never occurred to him to call security and ask them to seal the exits. How long had she been gone while he still ran panting and laughing to catch her? Like an idiot, he'd been calling her name, and chasing after a phantom.

Still holding the textbook, Foster positioned himself in front of the arriving car.

The doors slid aside and she lunged forward, almost colliding with him. Stopping short, she fell backward. Slid down to the carpeted floor. Curled herself into a defensive ball, sobbing, "Please, Dad!" Sobbing, "Don't."

Foster drew the pistol from inside his jacket and put the muzzle of it very gently against the top of her head. That wonderful dark hair. He said, "You're not my kid. ...And you're no actor." To seal the deal, to really make her despise him, he added, "You're a whore. A two-bit, dirty, cock-sucking whore."

She stopped crying and tilted her face up until the gun was aimed between her eyes. Any fear there had been replaced by fury. Whether or not he killed her, this Lucinda wanted to kill him. That was good. That was perfect.

From Oscarpocalypse Now *by Blush Gentry (p. 45)*

People, they loved Mitzi Ives. Loved her. Even after the FBI discovered that room packed full of money, people could still give her the benefit of the doubt. She lost her mother as a little baby. Her dad ran out during her teens, but Mitzi, she never went under. Maybe because her life was so hard, she turned out a survivor, you know?

Of course people started rumors. Anytime a woman, a single young woman makes it in Hollywood, the haters are going to trash-talk her. They'll say she fucked her way to the top in Foley work. Either that, or haters say she's a sadistic serial killer. They still say that. Rumors, I never paid any attention to.

No, my passion is chromium diopside. Why buy into all the haters and their jealousy when you can flaunt all the glamour of old Hollywood at a price point that makes our jewelry the best investment a swank, savvy, fashion-forward woman can own? Our motto is: *More Emerald than Emeralds.* But let a strong, smart woman get to the lead position in any industry and the legacy media will say she got there by torturing people to death. Just look at Sheryl Sandberg.

For those haters who say Mitzi Ives was a killer, I have just one question. "What happened to the bodies?" Show me all those dead bodies.

Jimmy hated sitting in the middle. The people, he complained, the ones seated behind them would kick his seat by accident. The ones sitting on either side would elbow him without thinking, or they'd whisper. The people sitting in the row in front of him would be too tall. No, the center of any theater might be the best viewing location from which to watch a movie, but the benefits were outweighed by the distractions. This was the reason home theaters were exploding.

"Tonight will be different," Mitzi told him. "Trust me."

Jimmy didn't understand about the rough cut. About the screening of the rough cut. He was just excited to get a pass onto the studio lot. She'd tried to dampen his spirits by explaining. This was no tuxedo-and-klieg-lights event. They'd be watching the prerelease cut of a Civil War picture. And not a particularly good one. And no one would be dressed any better than any casual Friday.

Not that Jimmy knew what a casual Friday was. The best he could muster was a clean do-rag wrapped around his caked dreads.

Why they'd been invited to this shindig, Mitzi couldn't fathom. Every evening was a choice between reading a classic book or going out to an industry event. In brief: whether to spend her time with smart dead people or alive idiots.

In the lobby of the studio's theater no one ventured near them. As if an invisible shield held them back, nobody approached her or addressed them. It might've been the bruises on her neck or the halfhearted way she'd applied concealer to her fractured nose and swollen eyes, but she knew she was a pariah for bigger reasons.

Here, every hello was a request for a job, either a job-job or a blow job. Mitzi could accept the fact that she was everyone's dirty little secret. Like a child star they'd all fucked the second before she was legal.

Jimmy was stupid not to see what she was. She hated him for his blindness, but she still wanted to be seen as something not corrupt. Even if right now he was ogling a nearby actress. The blonde wore a strapless gown so wired and boned that it made her breasts look like something being served on a tray. Her lashes were so loaded with mascara that her eyes looked like two Venus flytraps.

Jimmy, just dirty and unkempt enough to pass as a millionaire celebrity, leered at the woman. "Is that Blush

Gentry?" He sloshed his drink in the direction of the younger middle-aged blonde, a woman who fit somewhere between trophy wife and soccer mom. Her curls brought to mind drive-in movies. A generation of movies where a monster or mental patient had stalked and eventually killed her. The blonde curls still looked good. The waist was almost the same waist. As if she sensed Jimmy's leer, her blue eyes found him.

Mitzi knew the dance. In a moment Blush Gentry would break away from her conversation with an assistant nobody, and she'd make a beeline to see if Jimmy offered a better prospect for a new role. Yesterday's drug connection was today's executive producer. The marijuana industry was bankrolling independent projects, big projects, just as a means to launder the profits no bank would accept. Jimmy, with his neck tattoos and pockmarks, looked just the type to have a project to cast.

Straightaway, the actress locked her gaze on him and approached them. "Hi," she said, extending a beautiful hand, a hand that had once been lopped off with a meat cleaver. "I'm Blush."

Starstruck, Jimmy's pitted face flushed. His tattooed hand met her not-severed hand. "I'm Jimmy."

Although Blush didn't acknowledge her, Mitzi offered her hand. "Mitzi Ives." Adding, "Ives Foley Arts."

The actress touched hands with Mitzi, not making eye contact, and said, "Thanks, but I do all my own screaming."

Give it a minute and the actress's business card would appear, complete with links to her online highlights reel. And Jimmy would reciprocate with a screenshot of his GED. A big-shot mogul he was not. At that, his new best friend would get busy working the crowd for a better job prospect.

People saw Mitzi and looked straight through her until an industry tub made passing eye contact, all belly and whiskers. She told Jimmy, "I've got to do business." And headed for the foyer and the toilets.

In the women's room she stood at the sink and watched the door behind her in the mirror. The her in the mirror looked back with busted, bloodshot eyes. The industry tub walked in without hesitation. Looking around to make certain the place was otherwise empty, he said, "Word is you have something special you're auctioning."

The trend was that people consumed their media alone. Minus the ready laughter of others or the screams of an audience, the magic just didn't happen. Studios knew this. As did distributors and theater chains. That's why they held so-called contests and gave out free tickets to press screenings. Young people who felt they'd won something would be euphoric. Who better to pack the house with when a handful of local critics would be watching?

The shared limbic high of so many people, it almost guaranteed a spate of good reviews. The human limbic system needed community to reach its peak highs and lows.

But now home theaters and downloads meant more

people, particularly cultural arbiters and people with disposable income, the early adopters, were cocooning alone. Watching alone, and wondering why films weren't as funny or as scary or sad as they used to be.

Alone with Mitzi in the ladies' toilet, the industry tub asked, "Can I give it a listen?"

As she cued the file, Mitzi said, "I call it *Gypsy Joker, Long Blonde Hair, Twenty-Seven Years Old, Tortured to Death, Heat Gun.*" She watched as the industry tub fitted the buds into his hairy ears.

Everyone felt self-conscious expressing emotion alone. They needed a scream that gave them permission to scream. They needed to feel part of a larger limbic system. The way all dogs howled, that was limbic resonance.

Producers were locked into a battle for the best scream.

Mitzi pressed Play.

The industry tub jerked fully upright as if jolted with electricity. His body shook, and his eyes went so wide the whites showed in a bulging, bloodshot margin around each yellow iris.

She left him leaning forward, his hands braced against the edge of the sink, squeezing out anguished tears. She said, "Bidding stands at a million two."

At the bar the inevitable had taken place. Jimmy stood alone.

"What?" he asked. "Do I stink or something?" It was clear he was hurt. Blush Gentry had escaped, and no one else would go near him. Jimmy just didn't know how to live on the outside. Shunned by polite society: a feeling Mitzi had adjusted to years before.

It was hard not to love a man who so steadfastly ignored the awful truth about her. But it was even more difficult to respect him.

Mitzi led him into the small auditorium, where the center seats were clearly occupied. These, the best seats, were filled with small parties of people, or couples, with only a few single seats left empty among them. Mitzi left Jimmy on the aisle and edged her way down a center row. She excused her way past people until she arrived at a single seat smack-dab in the middle of everyone.

Jimmy had suggested they stay in and fuck. Thanks to the Ambien, every time felt like her first with him. If he wore a rubber, she had no idea. Probably not. He'd made nothing of his life, so the best he could imagine was to conceive another of himself. A do-over: Jimmy 2.0. As if to give himself a second shot, and doing so would shift the burden to this new him and give the current Jimmy permission to squander what was left of his years.

No doing, Mitzi had told him. No way was she getting knocked up.

As she sat in that centermost seat, the party of four sitting to one side of her rose and silently moved to distant seats. At that, a couple to her other side rose and relocated to less desirable seats. Within a few minutes of her arrival the area around Mitzi was vacant. Several rows ahead and behind her as well as wide margins of seats on either side were empty. She looked over at Jimmy and waved for him to join her.

"Lucky us," she called loudly. "I found two seats together!" The question of the rubber wouldn't leave her mind. To make matters worse was her dress, now the waist seemed tight. And the bodice. At that, Mitzi settled into her seat, heavy with the dread that she was no longer alone in her body.

The internet wasn't any help. She'd gotten remarried. Changed her name. Foster called her old work, and they told him as much. No one there had ever known her, not back then. Staff turnover. The last person he wanted to call was her dad.

Online he pulled up an obituary for her mother. It listed the survivors, and among them was Amber. Amber Jarvis, these days. Lucinda's mother. Directory assistance had a Jarvis but unlisted.

Finally, Foster caved in and called her father. Lucinda's grandfather.

"Hello?" Amber's dad sounded so chipper that Foster almost hung up. Why spoil such a good mood?

Foster pushed on. "Paul?"

Still sounding upbeat, the voice asked, "Is that you, Gates?"

He didn't ask about Amber, not right off the bat. First he tried to explain the ceremony the group had set up.

The latest trend was to buy an all-white casket, steel or lacquered hardwood. High gloss. All mourners would get a customized Sharpie with which to autograph the sides and lid of the coffin and to write a loving message. Foster tried to explain about the fake funeral. How it would provide closure, according to the parents group.

He tried to make it sound not crazy. More like a real thing done by enlightened people.

Amber's dad, Paul, stayed quiet. He wasn't buying it.

Foster said, "I'm sorry about Linda." He meant Amber's mother, dead of cancer as of three years ago according to the obituary. "I would've come," he offered.

Paul's tone wasn't angry, but he said, "Amber said not to tell you. She didn't want you there."

Foster said he understood. He didn't understand. He asked if Paul would come to the casket ceremony.

The older man waited a swallow and said, "Gates, I don't think so."

Foster wanted to explain about catharsis. What the group had drilled into him. About how the music and the flowers would provide a public setting for grief. He could externalize his loss instead of shouldering the burden alone. He wanted to explain about closure.

Instead he waited and held his tongue. More words would just be a way to keep Paul from eventually saying "No."

Perhaps out of pity, the man on the phone told him, "I'll tell her."

Foster said, "Thank you."

His former father-in-law added, "But, understand, she won't be there, either."

Mitzi could anticipate how a stranger would scream. She'd done this work so long and so often. In airports, she'd spy someone. In the supermarket. She knew who would scream for his mother, and who would only scream. Experience, at least hers, showed that no one screamed for God. Fat or thin. Black or white or Asian. Men or women, young or old, she knew how their final moments on Earth would sound.

On sight, she knew whether a stranger at the library would let loose with a full-throated giving up compared to a teeth-gritting, stubborn, grunting death. Or the worst, the mewling of a leaky balloon, something almost laughable, like a dog's squeak toy. Actual people actually died that way, a few.

And if she hadn't worked directly with such a person, she had her studio collection to fill in the blanks. The collection she'd inherited. Rows and rows of file cabinets, filling room after room, they held samples going back to the earliest forms of sound recording. Among them, tin foil wrapped around metal cylinders and banded with the hill-and-dale imprints of a stylus. A yellowed-paper tag tied to one cylinder read: *Recent Irish Immigrant Man, Chest Crushed, Basalt Millstone.* Tucked away were the machines that could still play such relics. Mitzi had picked through drawers filled with hollow cylinders of hardened wax. *Iroquois Squaw Strangled, Slow Middle Distance, Leather Cord.* She'd spend weeks exploring rooms filled with hard rubber and celluloid disks. Shellac disks and finally vinyl.

Such a trove of screams, it made her wonder whether films were invented simply as a medium to display them. Here was a sort-of immortality, agony preserved, archived and curated. She wondered if Native Americans were right. If a photograph could steal a person's soul, perhaps these recordings were the souls of the dead. They were dead but not in heaven or hell. They were inventory. They were making money. Some were—most were warehoused. Property cached away, here in these sliding metal drawers in these chilly concrete rooms.

This commodification of pain.

She'd pour a glass of Riesling. Sip enough to swallow an Ambien. Keep the bottle beside her for refills.

Each recording was a drug. Each made her heart beat faster. Her breathing slowed until she'd be forced to gasp for air. Each scream spiked her blood with adrenaline and endorphins. Slumped over the mixing console, her head clamped in earphones, she'd sit. Scream surfing.

Only at the end of her strength would she cue up her favorite. The master recording of her favorite: *Little Sister, Dies in Terror, Calls for Father.* She poured herself another glass of wine. She pressed Play.

* * *

His hand throbbed. The bite had become infected, the bite on his thumb from the airport. If he didn't keep his elbow bent, if he allowed his hand to hang low, it swelled up like a mitt and dripped something.

The doctor from his support group, Dr. Adamah, asked those present to bow their heads. Adamah was supposed to read the twenty-third psalm from the book of Psalms. But by glaring mistake he read from the book of Joshua, the account of Jericho's destruction. Not that anyone seemed to notice, the onlookers smiled raptly and nodded their approval.

Dr. Adamah wrapped up his reading, " …the men gave a loud shout, the wall collapsed…and destroyed…every living thing in it—men and women, young and old… " He closed his Bible, and the doctor motioned for Foster to take his place.

Standing at the podium, Gates Foster began to deliver the eulogy. His swollen hand raised as if he were testifying. With the exception of the few faces he recognized from the group, the entire assembly of mourners were strangers to him. Each stared until he flinched and looked away. In every direction he found the unblinking eyes of strangers who whispered to each other behind lifted hands. Someone giggled.

That's when Foster saw her. Amber. Amber Jarvis, now. Seated in a folding chair at the end of the chapel's back row was Lucinda's mother. It had been a long shot, but she was at the funeral. Alone, it seemed, she'd come.

Wearing a tan coat that was easy to spot in that sea of funeral black.

"When Lucinda was six," he began, "she asked her mother how to cook." He risked a look at the woman in the back row. She nodded for him to continue. "They were going to cook a roast for dinner…" A smile flitted across Amber's face as she saw where the story was going.

Foster paused and smiled back at her for a beat. "They took the roast out of its wrapping paper, and her mother asked Lucinda to get the pan out of the bottom cabinet." Each action and detail moved him to the next memory. "Her mother placed the roast on the cutting board and slid a knife from the knife block and explained that the first step was to slice about two inches off the smaller end of the roast." Saying this, Foster found his hands placing an invisible chunk of raw meat on the podium in front of him. His swollen hand straightened as if to make a karate chop, becoming the knife.

As he cut the invisible pot roast, he recounted how Lucinda had asked why they needed to shorten the roast. Her mother answered automatically that the smaller end cooked too quickly and would serve up dry and inedible, so it had to be set aside and cooked separately.

Foster laughed. "Lucinda didn't buy it." She'd asked why and kept asking why the entire roast wouldn't cook at the same rate. "That's how smart a kid she was," he said, even though it hurt to talk about his child in the past tense.

Behind him, now, the casket lay open, heaped with worn toys. Robb and the group had sent a whopping big casket spray of white carnations. Like something you'd throw over the back of a winning racehorse. A second-grade photo of Lucinda, smiling, enlarged to poster size, sat on an easel beside the casket.

Foster glanced up to meet the eyes of his ex-wife. A woman with her daughter's heavy, dark hair combed down her back, but threaded with gray along the sides of her face. She nodded, and he continued.

"Lucy never bought the reason for trimming the pot roast," he recounted. Her mother had offered other reasonable explanations. The smaller end tended to be too fatty, for example. The bit they trimmed away always served up too bitter or too tough. Whatever the case, her mother had reasoned, this was how she'd been taught by her mother, Lucinda's grandmother, so this was how she meant to teach her own daughter.

"And still"—Foster shrugged and offered up both hands helplessly—"Lucinda insisted they call her grandmother and keep asking."

So they'd called Lucinda's grandmother. A woman dead of cancer for three years now. And they'd asked why it was so important to trim the smaller end off the pot roast.

Here he wound up to deliver the story's payoff.

"It wasn't because the meat cooked unevenly or dried out," he said. "It was because the only roasting pan they'd had—so long ago—had only been so-big."

A lesson in perpetuating a mistake across generations. A dozen valid reasons, all wrong.

Lucinda, their smart, beautiful daughter had been the skeptic who'd brought their family to the final truth.

He looked up to see Lucinda's mother listening intently.

Among the seated mourners more telephones rose to record his words as Foster pressed forward. A small voice in the crowd said, "Harsh, dude," but faintly. Another small voice, the shout of a tiny man said, "He's not your daddy."

A laugh rippled through the chapel. The bereaved hunched forward, touching buttons, texting.

A louder voice, a man's voice, shouted, "That man is a child pornographer!" It was Foster himself. It was his voice, shouting from a different phone, "You don't have to be his sex slave. Not anymore."

They were watching the airport video. Someone was. It had gone viral and made him a freak show celebrity, and they'd found him.

So many phones were recording, watching to catch his reaction. And Foster craned his neck and struggled to see past the forest of raised arms. To see Lucinda's mother, but where she'd sat was an empty chair. Amber had fled.

Truncated bits of his voice shouted, "Pot roast!" Shouted, "Pot roast!" Somebody laughed and others shushed him because they were still recording. People wanted an encore.

Lucinda was dead, but no one cared. Lucinda had lived,

but no one cared. Building inside him was the rage he felt when he dreamed of beating down child molesters. The machine-gun him.

Bumping inside his jacket, like a heavy weight bouncing against the thud of his heart, was the gun.

Mitzi went to the window in her nightgown. Her new headache proved she wasn't dead. As did Jimmy snoring behind her. In the office building across the way only one window glowed. A single night owl like herself, the dad-shaped nobody studied something on his computer screen. A celebration it had to be. He was slugging back a whiskey-looking something from a bottle of something brown. Slugging it straight from the bottle.

Unseen, she toasted him with her own sticky glass of wine.

Jimmy simply wasn't working out. Not that he hadn't tried. He'd literally stood on her neck without breaking it. Stood balanced on one foot, even. And all she had to show for it was a sore neck, not so much as a slipped disk. She'd have to plumb deeper depths, maybe drive as far as Bakersfield or Stockton to find a replacement. Go trawling weight rooms for a steroid case. Her busted nose notwithstanding, Jimmy hadn't the killer instinct.

Behind her a snort sounded. The snoring from her bed stopped.

Jimmy, leathery, long-legged Jimmy with all of his

Riverside bad-boy swagger and hustle, he said, "You okay, baby?"

Mitzi didn't turn to face him, but she asked, "Would you like to be in a movie?" It wasn't her imagination, her breasts had grown. Her nipples had started to ache.

He told her, "Don't shit me." But his voice had a smile in it. There was so much silence around him she knew he must be frozen in disbelief.

She studied the man in the office. He tapped his keyboard and squinted into the glow of the monitor. She asked, "Do you know what the Goofy holler is?"

"Yeah," Jimmy lied.

"It's a yodel recorded by an Austrian ski racer named Hannes Schroll," she explained, "first used in a 1941 cartoon called *The Art of Skiing*." The yodel had since been used in hundreds of films and thousands of television productions and video games. It's quite possibly the most famous recording of a human voice. Schroll never earned a cent from it.

Jimmy shifted on the bed. Springs squeaked. "Never heard of the man," he said.

Mitzi sighed. "My point, exactly."

"Well," he huffed, "if I'm going to work, I'm going to get paid for it." He fumbled something and it slipped off the bedside table. Glass broke. An ashtray or stemware. Mitzi heard the snap of a cigarette lighter and smelled smoke drifting her way. The Fontaine was a smoke-free co-op, but he already knew that.

Mitzi gauged how much wine was left in her glass.

And then, there, afloat in the lonely well-lit office across the street, the man heaved forward in his chair. His glasses slid from his nose, and he vomited onto his desk.

Tonight he'd hide in his office. Tomorrow Foster would be arrested for the funeral. He'd surrender himself to the police. On every news website he was tonight's top story. On video after video, each shot from a different distance and angle, each video shot from some phone at the funeral, he withdrew the gun from his jacket. On his computer screen the tiny video version of him wheeled on the crowd, his arms straight out in front of him, the gun clutched in both hands. Folding chairs clattered and fell backward, spilling each row of people into the laps of the row behind. Mourners climbed each other, clawing away at a kicking pile of legs and thrashing arms. Through the computer's tinny speakers came their wails and the rip of yanked fabric pulled to shreds. Fingers grabbed collars and belts like rungs on a ladder. Shoes stomped over the layer of fallen, flattened bodies. On a different video the casket teetered on its stand, teetered and tipped, tipped and crashed to the floor spilling Teddy bears and sympathy cards.

On a third video the tiny Foster backed away from the screaming crowd and ducked out a fire exit.

Tonight he'd drink Jack Daniel's and surf the dark web one final time in search of his child.

At times he'd hated her for running away, even in a game

of tag. If she hadn't dashed into an elevator, regardless of her intentions, she'd still be here. So perhaps the funeral had accomplished its purpose. It had forced him to express his sorrow and his anger, and now both were gone. He'd overcome his addiction to her.

This indifference, it wasn't numbness because numbness implied the opposite: that some feeling would return. This had no opposite.

An email chimed in his inbox. A link from an address he didn't recognize. From a secret pervert or not, this was an ordinary link to a movie pirated on YouTube.

Foster was old enough to realize that no problem was entirely his own. What kept him awake at night also kept a million others up. The video was an excellent example. A fake high school cheerleader stumbled through a fake forest in implied darkness, barefoot and wearing only a lace negligee. The fake blood smeared on her hands and face was laughable. Generations had watched so much fake death. Beautifully lighted, badly acted, underscored with music. Now nobody could believe in the reality of death.

After people had been fed so many lies they'll never swallow anything as the truth.

Millions had watched the scantily clad actor push her way through briars and branches as a shadowy figure carrying a butcher knife stalked her. Foster wasn't the only person not buying it. He lifted the bottle of Jack Daniel's and put it to his lips. Drinking, yes, but not drunk.

No, this new indifference wasn't from whiskey. This was a complete inability to believe in anything.

The cheerleader struggled with her negligee snagged on something. Snagged on a thorn.

Her stalker lifted the knife so that the long blade caught the moonlight. Shining clean.

The cheerleader raised her hands to ward off the attack. She gasped.

The knife slashed down clean, but rose again smeared with blood. Stabbed downward bloody, but arose dripping.

In profile, the cheerleader's face tilted back, outlined against the full moon. Her glossy mouth moved. Her lips not matching the scream. The overdubbing was so bad, but the scream made up for it. The shrill voice of a terrified girl shrieked, "Help me! Daddy, please, no! Help me!"

The words seemed to hang in the air like so much smoke. If the cheerleader escaped, Foster didn't notice. If she died, he couldn't say.

It wasn't Lucinda's voice until it was.

He tucked his chin and vomited across his keyboard.

PART TWO:
TAPE BLEED

When the trumpets sounded, the army shouted, and at the sound of the trumpet, when the men gave a loud shout, the wall collapsed.

Book of Joshua 5:20

Jimmy's skin smelled like paint. So much so that when she'd wrap her hand around his dick and jerk it up and down—like shaking a can of spray paint—she'd half expect to hear something rattle inside. Ketoacidosis, the smell probably was, his body was that kind of lean. But Mitzi suspected years of vandalism had seeped into his pores, giving him body odor like so much late-night graffiti.

Who could guess what soup of chemicals the Rohypnol was interacting with in his bloodstream? Mitzi pulled open a file drawer and dug up some aerosol NARCAN given to her by Dr. Adamah for such emergencies. One whiff and Jimmy jolted eyes-wide, gasping awake.

He stammered, "Did I overdose?" His yellow eyes marveled at her. "You saved my life!"

Mitzi leaned in to adjust an RCA Type 77-DX ribbon mic, saying, "Don't thank me just yet."

The grave yawned, open and empty, at Foster's feet. Barely visible in the dark, tombstones stood like innumerable witnesses radiating outward from this spot. Each stone, granite or marble, a chunk hacked from the whole, impossibly big planet and hammered down to a uniform size and shape and made to carry a conventional message.

A framework was still in place atop the hole. Whether to cover the grave or to eventually lower Lucinda's casket, Foster couldn't tell.

The nighttime smell of cut grass took him back to childhood, while the left-behind bouquets, fresh and plastic alike, were without scent. In-ground sprinklers jetted ghosts of gray water into the still air.

A crunching reached him. Footsteps along a gravel path. Then a figure, a black outline, moved against the background of the blue night. A voice hissed, "Foster?" A male voice. And Robb came forward clutching an edge of each stone he passed like a blind man negotiating a strange room.

Instead of calling a lawyer, Foster had once more called his group leader. Hadn't Robb talked him out of that beef at the airport? Not that even Robb could disappear a weapons charge so easily. On the web, after the cheerleader movie had ended, a pop-up teaser had announced, "Bereaved father threatens mass shooting at daughter's funeral."

According to the web, Foster was dodging an arrest warrant. His cell phone pinged his every step, so he'd taken out the battery. The last thing he needed was jail time. Not after he'd heard Lucinda. Her voice, not his imagination. Not a dream. Her shout had shocked him sober, and he needed help. He needed some help.

"Thanks for coming," he said.

Robb said, "I should've called the police."

Foster lowered his voice. "Some amazing magic is at work here, my friend."

Robb looked at his wristwatch. "It's late."

Standing there at the grave intended for his daughter, Foster pressed his case. He insisted that none of this had happened by accident. Just the other day he'd been back to the airport to collect the suitcase that had flown to Denver without him. The little girl at the airport had been a sign. An omen. Sending his suitcase away so he could retrieve it, now, when he really needed it. It all seemed so predestined. Inevitable.

It was a divine something guiding him to reunite with Lucinda. Or it was his child's soul demanding resolution and revenge. But something, something had been directing his path.

He could see Robb wasn't buying it.

Foster proposed writing a check. A check for every dollar he had in the bank. Making it out to Robb. Robb only needed to cash it and deliver the cash to him. With cash Foster could buy a junker car off the web. Live in it. Sleep in it. Not transfer the title and drive it to pieces as he searched out Lucinda's scream in the movie.

Before he could ask, Robb said, "Nothing doing." He didn't need an aiding and abetting charge on his record. Not with his own past.

Foster pulled the gun from his pocket. "Walk with me?"

Jimmy had yet to realize that he was naked. His beef jerky body, corded with muscle, was tied spread eagle to a waist-high wooden platform. The usual audience of microphones crowded around him. Others hung by cords, close above his face.

Mitzi had tied a long strand of piano wire to a hook in the studio ceiling. This led down to where a small noose lay against his sunken belly. She looped the noose around the top of his scrotum and cinched it snug. *That he did notice.* Her touch immediately produced an erection.

At the mixing console she poured herself a glass of

pinot gris and tossed back an Ambien. She asked, "Did you know even dogs have laugh tracks?"

As she stretched her hands into a pair of latex gloves, Mitzi described how animal studies had identified the way dogs pant while at play. Analysis with a sonograph shows the panting includes bursts of various frequencies. These are similar to the high-frequency "chirping" rats produce during rough play and sex.

Mitzi bundled her hair under a surgical cap, saying, "Both the chirping and the panting seem to function as laughter." When researchers recorded the specialized panting and played it back to anxious dogs confined at animal shelters, this canine laugh track prompted tail wagging. The recorded laughter triggered face licking. Dogs abandoned stress-related behavior such as pacing, and those same dogs began to play.

She flicked a fingertip against a can mic and watched the needle on the corresponding meter. "Yawning and laughter," she went on to explain, "are contagious because they were the protohuman's method for regulating the mood of their group or tribe."

Jimmy's eyes drifted closed. He appeared to be slipping back into dreams.

"A major trait of psychopaths," she explained, "is that they don't yawn when people around them yawn. Psychopaths don't feel empathy. They lack the mirror neurons."

She placed a gloved hand on a cold metal handle and

cranked it a half rotation. The handle drove squeaky gears. The mechanism was archaic and rusty and hadn't been used. At least not in her time. She muscled it, and the platform lowered until the wire to the ceiling drew taut.

As she fitted earplugs into her ears, Mitzi thought vaguely about Odysseus plugging the ears of his crew with wax, then lashing himself to a ship's mast so he alone could listen to the Sirens. It was typical, how a mere sound could lure people to their doom.

Jimmy blinked awake and looked at her with confused eyes.

She turned the crank another half rotation. The table edged lower. He'd soon get the picture.

As she tried to explain it, the platform would lower while Jimmy's wrists and ankles would stay bound at the original height. If he could keep his entire body rigid, the noose wouldn't pull tighter and do any damage. As long as he could hold all of his muscles tensed and keep his body hanging stiffly in space, he'd keep his testicles.

She poured another glass of wine and chewed a couple Ambien for faster effect. The meters bumped, their needles jumping in response to the slightest noise. Lastly, she fitted a pair of goggles over her eyes. In the event of blood spray. She donned noise-canceling headphones over her earplugs to complete her sphere of silence.

She wanted to tell Jimmy about the Grateful Dead. How they'd invented the phenomenon known as "tape bleed."

An early master tape of theirs had been wound too tightly, and magnetic coding from one section seemed to imprint on adjacent sections of the tape. This produced a ghostly reoccurring echo. An unintended overdubbing, this faint layer of sound in the wrong places. Like most accidents, it looked like a disaster at first. Soon everyone in music was trying to intentionally produce the same shimmering effect in their work.

She uncapped a felt-tipped pen and wrote on a DAT cartridge: *Riverside Thugster, Sudden and Traumatic Orchiectomy.*

Mostly, Mitzi was giddy. What with the wine and all. Jimmy? Timmy? She racked her brain, suddenly uncertain who this paint-smelling man strapped to her table was. How had they met?

At this rate she'd never remember turning the crank, lowering the table, leaving this stranger suspended in air by only the strength of his flexed muscles. With her eyes fixed on the console, she cranked and kept cranking, deaf to everything, forgetting how often she'd rotated the handle.

Even now, her headache was abating. With every uptick of the VU meters, the pain in her skull ebbed further away.

As all the meters pegged into the red, Mitzi felt a sting on her arm. As if a hornet had stung her just below the elbow. Already blood was wicking through the sleeve of her lab coat. Pulling back the cuff, she found something embedded in her skin. A chip of something green, sharp edged like a green flint arrowhead. She plucked it out and turned to pour herself another glass of wine.

Both the bottle and glass were gone. Of the wineglass, only the base and the stem remained, standing on the console where she'd set the glass down. Of the bottle, only the thick, green-glass bottom and some ragged portions of the body stood. The green arrowhead in her arm had been a shard of the bottle. It had burst. Both the bottle and the glass had exploded.

"Let me tell you a story, friend," said Foster. He waved for Robb to start down a row of graves. Foster jerked the gun for him to turn where needed. Without speaking, they arrived at a white headstone that almost glowed in the dimness. In this, a section dedicated to infants and children, some plots were heaped with toys. So many greeting cards and flowers were banked against one head-stone that they obscured the name. There the two men stopped and stood.

The dark hummed with crickets and tree frogs and the rustle of mice. The sound of things too fragile for the day-light. And the silence of the owls and snakes that preyed upon those most fragile.

"You were so worried about the quarterly audits," Foster said. He stood gazing down on the pale stone. "You decided to work through lunch. And then you decided to work late, so you called your wife, Mai, to pick up your kid at day care."

Foster knew the story by heart. He'd heard Robb tell it so often in the group. "That day the temperature hit a hundred," he continued. "Then Mai called from the day care to say Trevor wasn't there." The staff said Robb had never dropped the boy off. Robb had insisted he had. He charged that the day care workers were covering up something. Over the phone he shouted for Mai to call the police. He could hear her relaying his accusation and the staff members insisting Robb had never stopped by that morning.

Over the phone Mai asked if Robb had taken their son out of the backseat. They'd had the windows tinted. Even if someone had walked past, no one could see inside. Very quietly Mai told him to check the car.

Robb bent low over the tiny headstone and righted a glittery plastic wreath that had toppled.

"You stood above the spreadsheets that covered your desk," said Foster, "and you knew what you'd done." And if it had reached a hundred degrees that day, it had been so much worse inside a locked car parked among a few acres of cars on an open concrete parking lot.

Baby Trevor must've woken up alone still strapped in his car seat. And Robb would never know how much his child had suffered.

Mai had left him that day. First hysterical, then sedated to catatonia. The police, of course the police had come to arrest him on charges of reckless endangerment and negligent manslaughter. In short order the quarterly audits became the least of his worries. In part because he'd been fired for absenteeism. That, and the fact that everyone in the company had watched as he'd run to his car. They'd all watched first him, and later the paramedics, attempt the impossible with the small limp body. Foster asked, "You remember?"

The toys on the grave, Mai's relatives had left them. Foster didn't need to move the stuffed bear and the basketball to reveal who was buried here. Foster offered up the story not to torment Robb, but to remind him that Robb, himself, was also human. They were both human. And they would both fuck up on occasion.

"As brutal as that nightmare was," Foster said, "at least you know what occurred." Robb knew the full story to tell and tell to the group until it no longer hurt. Or hurt less. And that was more than Foster could claim.

The story. The grave. It was something Robb could grasp.

Foster added, "My friend." He pocketed the gun and produced the check. All the money he had in the world. The check he'd already written and stashed in his pocket, he handed it over.

And Robb took it.

Mitzi paced along the rows of filing cabinets. Her fingers trailed across the file drawers, each crammed with tapes recorded at least a generation before. The metal cabinets thick with dust. Dust muffled the sound of her footsteps on the concrete floor.

Under one arm she lugged an open shoebox. Juggling a wineglass in that same hand. Her head a little foggy from the wine, but intent on her hunt. Her other hand she dipped into rusted file drawers and rotting cardboard boxes. She examined *Girl Rider, Crushed, Stampeding Bison.* She wondered how someone had staged that scenario. *Surfer, Flayed Alive, Vampire Bats.* It boggled the mind. Both of these had been before her time.

When the shoebox was full or her wineglass was empty, she'd head back to the sound pit and play her selection.

The studio storerooms presented a hoarder's warren of stacked boxes patched with strapping. Heavy boxes had crushed those beneath them, spilling out reels of unspooling magnetic tape. A firetrap is what it posed. Flammable shellac. Hardened wax. Here and there trailed leftover movie scenes on silver nitrate stock, dubbed long ago by the predecessor of her predecessor of her predecessor and promptly forgotten. The fish-smelling, low-tide stink of decaying celluloid.

A match, even just a spark, and the entire trove would burn like the *Hindenburg.*

Mitzi considered the recorded phone calls left by people seated aboard hijacked jetliners doomed to crash. Those, and the voicemails left by people trapped above the fires in the World Trade Center. These messages were all over the web. People sounded so rational saying their good-byes and their I-love-you's to an answering machine. Especially considering how so many of those same people would be among the two hundred–plus who'd shortly jump to their deaths.

What moved Mitzi's heart was how the people who received those messages went on to treasure those tapes and duplicate them and to duplicate the duplicates to be certain those final words would never be lost.

That was always the impulse: To preserve, to curate. To cheat death.

Ambien did a great job of punching holes in her short-term memory. It was her long-term memory that was the problem.

What had it been like to be eleven years old? Twelve? If she couldn't sleep, her father would pile together a nest of old blankets in the middle of the sound pit. She'd curl into the nest, and he'd extinguish the lights. In that sound-less, lightless place he could delete the whole world. Then slowly he'd construct a new world around her. Seated at the mixing console he'd create the sound of wind. He'd add the crackle of logs in a fireplace. The sonorous tick-tock of an antique clock. The rattle of a loose pane in a leaded-glass window. Her father would build a castle around her and place her in the highest tower. Doing all of this with only sound, he'd place her in a canopy bed hung with embroidered velvet, and she'd fall asleep. That was her memory of being twelve.

Foster jerked awake. A dog's bark, or something like a dog's bark, had broken his sleep. Slumped in the driver's seat of a car, he found himself parked at the edge of a grassy yard. A rotund man tossed a baseball to a cap-headed little boy who tossed it back. Not a dog barking, the noise had been the slap of the leather catcher's mitt the kid wore.

His car was nosed into the curb. He'd parked at an angle to the lawn of an apartment complex, in one of a long row of diagonal parking spaces. The spaces on either side of his were empty.

Slouched as he was, Foster could see the man and the boy, but it was unlikely they could see him. The car he'd bought off Craigslist. Fifteen hundred dollars for a beater Dodge Dart with duct tape patching the seats, and a couple hundred thou on the odometer. An AM radio. The oil pan leaked. A fry cook in a fast-food uniform had signed over the title. They'd done the deal in the parking lot during the cook's lunch break. The tags were good for another ten months. Big bench seats meant he could sleep if he didn't get caught for vagrancy.

The fry cook said he trusted Foster to transfer the title. Fat chance of that.

Whoever had tinted the car's windows had done a lousy job. The blue film had bubbled and rippled until it felt as if he were underwater. Still, it was good enough to keep out unwanted attention.

According to the Internet Movie Database, the film dubbed with Lucinda's scream was called *Babysitter Blood-bath*. To his surprise the actress was a bit of a legend. Blush

Gentry, she'd played the pretty sidekick in a generation of horror films. Always the funny blonde sexpot, she'd cracked the jokes and denied there was a serial killer until she became his victim. In most of her roles she died with blood bubbling from her lovely mouth.

Most of Ms. Gentry's work had fallen from public awareness, but this one film still drew an audience.

Seventeen years ago, when she'd made the movie, she'd been twenty-four. That put her age at forty-one. A few years Foster's junior, but not many.

These days Blush Gentry paid her bills on the convention circuit. At Comic Cons and Wizard Worlds and Dragon Cons she charged for autographs and for posing with fans for pictures. She maintained a sizable following on social media.

The old man and the kid continued to toss the horsehide between them.

Intuition prompted Foster to activate his phone. He knew not to keep it on for long, not when any ping off a cell tower could bring a SWAT team down on him. He shuffled through his database of photos just to be certain.

It was the old man. Without question. The man playing catch was Otto Von Geisler, the notorious Belgian child pimp. Foster's proof was a low-resolution Interpol photograph of the monster's ear.

Foster weighed the risk as he unbuckled his seat belt. He slipped the gun from his shoulder holster. Big redbrick apartment houses and small lawns stretched in every direction.

His plan: Grab the kid. Save the kid and pistol-whip the predator.

A horn honked. A crackle of radio static and the hushed roll of tires brought another car into the space on the passenger side of his. A police cruiser, it nosed into the curb.

From where Foster slouched he could see only the rack of lights on the roof, but he heard the driver's-side door. Staying low, watching across the length of the front seat, he saw a uniformed patrolman step out and walk toward the game of catch.

A voice called out, "Hello, officer." The man, not the boy. Von Geisler's voice.

As Foster watched, the patrolman offered a phone to Von Geisler and said, "Sorry to bother you nice folks." He nodded to draw their gaze to the phone. "But have you seen the man in this picture?"

Von Geisler took the phone and studied it. The boy closed the gap between them and craned his neck to look. The monster elbowed the boy and said, "Looks like a mean hombre, don't he?" To the officer he said, "What's he wanted for?"

The officer said, "Assault with a deadly weapon." After a quick cautious glance at the boy, he added, "And knowingly receiving online images of an illegal nature."

Whoever had gotten into his office computer had known how to search better than Foster knew how to scrub.

* * *

The doctor said, "Congratulations." He was peering down into his stainless-steel sink. Studying a new mess of ashes scattered across the bottom.

The specter of pregnancy jolted Mitzi. Otherwise she felt like a normal person. Her hangover had passed, and she hoped that was the cause for congratulations.

It wasn't a child Mitzi wanted to avoid so much as the day she'd eventually have to tell the child the true nature of the family business.

At school, Mitzi, little Mitzi, insecure only-child Mitzi with no mother at home and only her father, she'd been a broken record. *My daddy makes movies. My daddy did the voice in that cartoon, in the part where the mermaid trades her tail for two legs, where she screams.* Kids being kids, her classmates had wanted to meet him. And he'd obliged them, allowing little girls to drop by his studio, the warren of concrete rooms. In the sound pit he'd made them close their eyes while he'd create a special effect. They'd shout out *Rain!* And he'd show them how rain was really the sound of ball bearings in a wooden box tipped to one side. *Thunder!* And thunder was a flexible sheet of aluminum waved in the air.

If they asked about the screams, he'd lie. He'd tell them that he hired actors who specialized in screaming. Then he'd have each little girl step up to a microphone, and he'd record her scream. When he played each scream back, they'd all laugh. It would sound so fake. Mitzi, too, would laugh. Back before she knew the truth.

Now she shuddered to think how easily her friends came to visit. The screaming and the laughing, afterward. Tension and release. One girl in a hundred would ask why the studio smelled like bleach, and Mitzi would shrug. To her that was just the smell of her father. He'd always smelled like bleach, his hands in particular. It had become a smell her nose no longer detected.

A snap. The doctor snapped his fingers. The noise jump-cut Mitzi back to the here and now. Sitting in the smoky examining room, the charred crud littering the bottom of the sink.

Dr. Adamah examined the ashes. One eyebrow arched almost to his hairline, and he asked, "Does the name James Fenton Washington ring a bell?"

What the doctor had dropped flaming into the sink was a stained bandanna. The red cloth smelled like acetate, like spray paint, even more than her bed did. Mitzi didn't understand why, but she'd sensed that it was the item to hand over.

The cloth had blazed up in a flash. In the sink, flames had crawled over it, blue flames coated it. The cloth had twisted like something in agony. Charred patches peeled away like the black skin of a snake. Like shed scales. Larger pieces shattered into fragments. Fragments broke into flakes and fizzled out with a last spiral of acrid smoke.

The doctor lifted a hand to the taps. He twisted one

and let the water run until steam rose from the sink. He moved a hand under the faucet, fanning his fingers to direct the water. Rinsing away the ash. Pumped liquid soap from a bottle and washed. He pulled paper towels from a dispenser on the wall. With clean, dry hands he turned to the electronic tablet on the counter and began to keyboard something. Not looking up, he said, "According to James you're not out of the woods yet."

Mitzi didn't respond because she really, really did not want to hear the answer.

Regardless, the doctor asked, "When did you have your last period?"

Bless the scalpers. Even here, lining the sidewalk outside the convention center, young men stood waving lanyards. From each loop of cord dangled a laminated badge. For three hundred in cash Foster procured something to hang around his neck, and that, that got him inside the doors.

Inside presented a new dilemma.

Not two steps into this melee, a uniformed security guard was stopping entrants. She directed each elf or pirate to extend his or her arms straight out sideways while she ran a wand up and down them. And not a magic wand, this was standard issue for detecting metal. Same as guards used at airports worldwide. The gun, Foster had stowed it in the loose, flopping top of his boot. Before he could retreat out the doors he'd just entered, the guard was already waving him forward.

"Arms up, please." Her tone was bored. Clearly, patting down mermaids and robots had long ago lost its charm.

Hers was an impossible task, to judge from the arsenal of ray guns and scimitars, crossbows, pitchforks, blunderbusses, muskets, fencing foils, daggers, spiked maces carried by knights, axes wielded by Vikings, the vampire killers armed with stakes and mallets, the Romans with broadswords, the hand grenades, claymores, staves, machetes, lances and pikes, the tridents, bullwhips, harpoons and tomahawks streaming into the building.

Foster resigned himself to getting busted. Busted and arrested. She ran the wand up the inside of his leg. The wand began to bleat.

"Sir," she said, "I'll need you to remove your boot." She moved back a step.

Foster stood on one foot and pulled off the boot. Something clattered on the concrete floor. The gun.

The guard hooked the wand to her belt and placed a hand on her own holstered revolver. "Put your hands on top your head," she said. She crouched to retrieve the gun. There was no mistaking it for a toy. What she didn't do is check the clip for bullets. She stood and stepped back and ordered, "With one hand, remove your mask, now." She unsnapped the guard on her holster.

If the crowds pressing past him noticed, no one reacted. Slow, with no sudden movement, Foster gripped the top of his executioner's hood and pulled it off.

The guard gave him a long look. She slipped a phone

from the back pocket of her slacks and held the screen near his face. Her eyes twitched between him and whatever image her phone displayed. "Here," she said, and handed him the gun. "You have a good convention."

Startled, Foster accepted the gun and started to thank her, but the guard was already shouting over his shoulder, "Next!"

Brainless wasn't bad. Today, brainless was right up her alley. This world of grunts and clanking iron, the same tasks repeated mindlessly until failure, Mitzi loved it the moment she'd stepped through the door of the weight room. The Sisyphean repetition of lifting and lowering. Nothing represented life better than this endless losing battle against gravity. The grunts and cries that conveyed so much more than words ever could.

Here was an assembly line where people manufactured themselves. On these weight benches and calf machines. With its pulleys and pull-up bars, this clanking room was something Henry Ford might invent. Or Louis B. Mayer. A conveyor belt for the mass production of gods and goddesses, where people were the workers and the product. Here they paid to sweat, performing bicep curls and leg extensions in the hope of becoming some dream version of a new self. Whether it was making a movie, frame by frame, or bodybuilding, it was only the results that most people saw. Or wanted to see. The actual labor was too deadening to watch.

Mitzi accepted a clipboard from the girl at the front desk. A standard insurance liability waiver. Where it asked, "Are you pregnant?" she checked the box marked NO.

A scream, a woman's ragged, choking scream made her jump with surprise.

One thick-legged behemoth was resting between sets in the squat rack. The scream had come from a phone he held sideways, his eyes glued to the screen.

Again the scream rang out. A woman. A woman's sobbing, rasping scream, it was a movie playing on his phone. The scream drowned out the grunts and clanks. It was some woman, begging, beseeching, "Please, no! You can't! I'm your wife!"

The scream stood Mitzi's hair on end and drew a cold finger down her back. She knew this one. It had been used in a cheap Halloween release years back, the kind of schlock shocker theaters rent to show at midnight on Friday the thirteenth. The movie's title was *The Warlock's Blood Feast*. The scream's formal title, written in her father's handwriting on a tape Mitzi had found by accident, was *Traitorous Woman, Dispatched Quickly, Rusty Ice Pick*. Mitzi had listened to it more times than she could count.

This scream was precious to her. It was her mother's.

Gates Foster flowed with the tide of costumed witches and spacemen. He let the mob steer him through the convention hall. There, booths showcased television programs and comics publishers. Huge banners hung from the rafters to tout blockbuster summer movie releases and video games. Everywhere he looked, Foster saw nothing but people massed together.

Somewhere in this maze of aisles divided by booths selling toys and tables where artists drew and autographed their work, somewhere was Blush Gentry. According to the convention program she'd be meeting her fans—for a fee. The program listed her in Hall K. Where that was, Foster had no idea.

He'd felt idiotic while buying the elements of his costume: the hood, the spandex leotard and tights, the boots and breastplate and ridiculous cape. The gloves. The store shelves had been picked almost clean by convention-goers, so he'd been forced to mix and match. His spandex sagged, or it bunched in the wrong places, showing the lines of his underwear and binding. The holes cut in the executioner's hood seldom aligned with his eyes, so he often stumbled over galactic storm troopers or hobbits. But here he wasn't foolish, in costume he was invisible.

The gun sunk lower in his boot. Its hardness bit into his ankle with every step. The hood trapped his breath and made his scalp itchy with sweat. A map printed on the back page of the program showed that Hall K would be to his right, and Foster tacked slantwise to cut in that direction through the lurching robots and staggering zombies.

He was always on the lookout for Blush Gentry, for her

trademark blonde curls. On pirated internet videos he'd seen her eaten alive by an army of rats. Since the dawn of films when young women had been tied to railroad tracks and tied to logs sent into huge sawmill blades, Hollywood had never lacked new ways to take pretty girls apart.

He found her line long before her. Long, long before. It snaked into Hall H, three halls away from where she sat at a folding table autographing glossy photos and chatting with her fans. It cost fifty dollars merely to receive a ticket and join the line. He hadn't gone three steps before another cache of fans had paid their money and fallen in behind him.

The place was a target-rich environment for any pedophile. Tens of thousands of children broke away from their parents and milled in awestruck wonder at the sight of their cartoon heroes. Everywhere, exits linked the halls to the outside world. Any pervert in a Teddy bear get-up could take his victim by the little hand and spirit her away without notice.

Foster tugged his eye holes into place and studied his phone, comparing his gallery of screen captures with people in the crowd. Not far from him, an astronaut removed his helmet and tucked it under one arm. The man's thin hair was plastered to his forehead with sweat, and his haggard face had flushed red from the heat. Not only did this middle-aged geek look out of place, he looked familiar.

Slyly, Foster brought his phone level with the man in the

near distance and quickly thumbed through old images. His nose, his chin, and his neck matched perfectly those of an otherwise pixilated face. Here was the answer.

Something tugged at his cape. A voice said, "Hey."

Foster turned to find a sandal-wearing gladiator with a spray of pimples swelling his cheeks. The gladiator asked, "What are you?"

A princess with fake braids coiled beneath her crown asked, "Who are you supposed to be?"

The astronaut-slash–child molester had struck up a conversation with a small girl dressed as a ladybug. The pair seemed alarmingly chummy.

He told the gladiator, "I'm nobody." The astronaut's nose at the very least looked to be an exact match. If Foster left the line to save the kid, he might never meet Blush Gentry. But in another beat the pervert could walk that tiny ladybug through any exit and into oblivion.

In line ahead of them, a legion of samurai and ninjas turned to give Foster a good looking-over. Someone took a step forward and they all took a step. They were all bored, flicking their phones and needing more distraction.

Foster directed their attention to the astronaut. "You see that man?" he asked. "Every year eight hundred thousand children are reported missing. That's according to the Center for Missing and Exploited Children…" He felt like a modern-day Fagin.

The assembled ninjas elbowed some masked highwaymen, and even more Scottish highlanders turned to where the astronaut was chatting up the ladybug. Foster continued, "That's more than two thousand kids a day. One kid gets kidnapped every forty seconds in America." He let the numbers sink in. "And that man is Emory Emerson." He held his phone for the princess and those close enough to see the image he had on file.

The listening company of centurions and zombies no longer looked bored. The princess asked, "So?" not taking her eyes off the astronaut. "Do something!"

Foster shrugged under his hood. "I can't make a move until he tries something."

A zombie asked, "You a cop?"

Foster squatted down, reached into his boot and withdrew the gun, just for a flash before tucking it back. His ankle burned where it had been rubbed raw. The crowd stared at the bite scar on his hand as much as the gun itself.

The pimply gladiator drew a plastic broadsword from his belt and said, "Maybe you can't do anything, but I can." He turned to the princess and said, "Save my place in line, okay?"

Standing on tiptoe, the princess kissed him on the forehead.

Before the gladiator had charged halfway to the astronaut, the samurai broke ranks to follow. The elfin bandits went to join the fray. A cry went up from the astronaut, a bellow of panic and confusion, as the swarm of musketeers and ghouls surrounded and enveloped him. The plastic

clack of fake cudgels and nunchucks drew even more attention. More people in line, dazed by boredom, stepped
away to video the ruckus.

Seeing his opportunity, Foster edged past the distracted
masses. As the ladybug screamed in alarm and the pervert
was pelted with foam rubber ninja stars, Foster made
his way through Halls I and J and into Hall K where
the object of his search sat alone and ignored for the
moment. Her handler had stepped away to call security, so
it seemed. Blush herself looked older than he'd expected,
almost his own age. Around her mouth were etched the
telltale lines of a heavy smoker. Her hair looked too bright
to be natural. She sat at the table holding a felt-tipped pen.
A pile of glossy photos was stacked at her elbow.

Blush Gentry looked up with a sweet smile and asked,
"Do you have a ticket?"

Foster fumbled inside the cuff of his spandex sleeve and
brought forth a paper ticket dark with sweat. He asked,
"Can we go somewhere? Somewhere and talk?"

She scribbled her name across a photo and handed it
toward him, saying, "Thank you for stopping by."

The line was re-forming. Any handler or talent wrangler
would be back in a moment. Panicked, Foster stooped
slightly, reached into his boot, and for the third time that
day took out the gun.

Mitzi caught sight of herself. No one could escape the
mirrors that lined the weight room from floor to ceiling.

Even her baggy sweatshirt suggested a small baby bump. In her mind lingered so many half memories and dream fragments soaked in blood. She couldn't definitively swear she had or had not gotten her period in the past several months. One half image stood out in particular, bleeding from her vagina. Or bleeding from someone's vagina. It hadn't hurt, and she'd put foam plugs into her ears, which didn't make sense. She'd plugged her ears and said a prayer just before her last period, and the words of the prayer had been: "Scrambled eggs...bacon...orange juice..." The garbled nonsense of a dream.

A chime sounded inside her gym bag. Her own phone. A producer, Schlo, was calling. She said a quick prayer that it was a dubbing job, but her prayer came out as, "Poached eggs...link sausage..."

"Mitz, my baby girl," Schlo said, "I need you should borrow me the original of that latest scream of yours." *Traumatic Orchiectomy.*

Mitzi cupped the phone in her hand to mask the clank of weights around her. "You know that's not my policy," she told him. The policy was to never relinquish the original recording of a scream. Besides, the original was as lost as all the screams in the studio archives. Near her a man bellowed under a bar loaded with iron plates the size of car tires. His huffing and growling competed with the loud clank of cast iron.

"What?" the producer shouted over the phone. "Are you in a factory? Are you a United Auto Worker these days?"

A memory haunted Mitzi with the words, "Pancakes…
oatmeal…toast." A prayer like a waitress reciting the menu
at a diner.

The phone said, "There's something wrong with that
last scream." Jimmy's scream.

Mitzi asked, "How do you know?"

"I'm texting you a link is how I know," Schlo said.
"We're one day into audience testing and—boom."

A new text chimed. Mitzi swiped to find a link. Clicking
on the link brought up an Associated Press wire story. The
headline read: "Over a Hundred Die Watching Film."

Foster had to give it to her. Blush Gentry was a trouper.
No sooner had he flashed the gun than she'd announced
to the crowd, "The talent needs to tinkle. Can you give
me a sec?" Her handler was just stepping up to assist her,
and she told the woman, "I'll be back in five." She put two
fingers to her mouth to mime smoking a cigarette.

Seeing the line that snaked away, the ever-growing
number of fans waiting for their moment, Foster had no
idea how to exit the floor.

"Give me your phone," Blush said and jerked her head
toward an unmarked door. She accepted his phone and
stepped away as if confident he'd follow. With every step
she was keying something into the small screen. Past the
door, they stood in a service corridor, cinder block walls,
fluorescent lights. There, she reached to tug at the hem of
his executioner's hood, saying, "Give me this."

He pulled it off, ashamed of how heavy it was with his sweat.

She took it with two fingers. Her lips curled in disgust. "This thing stinks," she said, then took a deep breath and flipped the damp cloth over her head.

Foster started, "I just need to ask you a couple — "

She cut him off. "How do you think I'd look in a burka?" She lifted her chin until her eyes met his through the holes cut in the black cloth. Startling against the black cloth, her blue eyes darted sideways.

He looked for what she might be indicating. A security camera watched them from the passageway ceiling. He asked, "A what?"

"It worked for Elizabeth Smart," she said, once again thumbing the keys of his phone. With her quick, confident gait, she was leading him down the corridor to a door marked Exit. Beyond that, they stepped into an alley. Without slowing, drawing no notice, her wearing the black hood and him clutching his cape to hide the gun in his hand, they followed the alley to a street.

Blush asked, "You got a car?"

Foster pointed, "This way. But I only need to ask a question."

She strode off in the direction he'd indicated.

"Wait," Foster protested. "Where are you taking me?"

Her ability to text and walk at the same time was extraordinary. "You ever hear of Aimee Semple McPherson?" she asked. "How about Agatha Christie?"

They were approaching a parking structure. "Here," Foster said and nodded toward the elevator. He pressed the Up button and the memory of the escort girl, the surrogate Lucinda, came to mind. The doors slid open and they stepped inside. He pressed the button for the floor.

As they rode upward, still intent on her keyboarding, her voice muffled by the hood, Blush said, "Both Aimee and Agatha hit mid-career slumps, you know?" She said, "I know all about mid-career slumps."

The elevator stopped and they stepped out. The concrete ramps sloped away, crowded with parked cars. Foster slid a hand down inside his spandex tights, feeling for the keys he carried in his shorts.

Blush's eyes didn't leave his phone as she continued to talk and text. "It was 1926, okay? McPherson was the most famous religious leader in America, but she was losing her edge, you know?" She followed as he led her along the rows of cars. "Agatha Christie was a writer with mediocre sales..." Her voice trailed off.

Foster arrived at the car, the Dodge Dart from Craigslist. He opened the passenger side door, and Blush climbed in still wearing the hood.

As she explained it, both women had disappeared without a clue. McPherson for a month. Christie for ten days. Both had been the subject of worldwide searches and intense media coverage. Thousands of volunteers had combed the globe trying to find them. "No offense to

Jesus," Blush said, "but disappearing and reappearing is a woman's version of death and resurrection. A miracle, you know?"

Behind the wheel, Foster prompted, "Do you remember a movie called *Babysitter Bloodbath*?"

As she clicked her seat belt, she said, "Get driving."

He asked, "Don't you need to go back?"

She dug in the pocket of her jacket and brought out a pack of cigarettes. With the hood hiked up to uncover her mouth, she put one between her lips and pressed the car's cigarette lighter. Talking around the cigarette, she said, "Just drive."

He wanted to tell her not to smoke, but there were bigger issues at stake.

She pressed a final key on the phone and said the word, "Send."

As she explained it, Aimee Semple McPherson was believed to have drowned off a beach near Los Angeles. Agatha Christie was widely thought to be a victim of murder, most likely by her husband who wanted a divorce so he could marry his secretary. When eventually found, McPherson claimed to have been kidnapped and taken to Mexico. Christie claimed amnesia. But both women were welcomed back with enormous fanfare. Thousands came to greet them. Their lagging careers rebounded to make them enduring worldwide successes.

As Foster turned the key in the ignition, he could hear sirens in the distance.

"Drive," Blush ordered. "You don't want to get caught, not so soon."

The sirens grew louder. Closer.

Foster craned his neck to look back as he pulled out of the parking space.

"I'll answer all your questions," Blush said. She puffed her cigarette. "But only so long as you keep me kidnapped."

The car was already spiraling down toward the exits. Foster protested, "But I'm not kidnapping you."

Blush countered, "I need the career boost. You need whatever."

The car lurched to a stop at the exit gate. Foster had prepaid but hesitated before pressing the button and inserting his receipt. Shaking his head, he said, "You can't make me kidnap you."

Blush lifted his phone near her face. From it she read, "Dear 9-1-1. I've kidnapped the beautiful and wildly talented actress Blush Gentry." She paused, her eyes smirking.

Foster inserted the ticket and pressed the button. The gate swung open.

From Oscarpocalypse Now *by Blush Gentry* (p. 50)

People say I staged my own kidnapping because I knew about the Academy Awards, about what would happen at the Oscars that year. People also say certain jewelers and fashion designers refused to lend jewels and clothes for the occasion. That puts me in very good company. People who make these accusations overlook the fact that I was being pistol-whipped.

These same people insist a new weapon called Dustification was used to powderize the World Trade towers. Look up *dustification*. There's your answer. I'm sorry if my kidnapping doesn't fit the narrative of a bunch of black helicopter kooks.

Mitzi poured another glass of wine and toasted Jimmy's memory. The deal with dating conceited men like him was that she'd hoped some of his excess self-esteem would rub off. Women always secretly hoped this: that dating a narcissist would give them confidence by osmosis. It never worked.

She lifted an edge of the bandage on her forearm. The wound from the shard of wine bottle had almost healed. It wouldn't even leave a scar.

She glanced back at the noose hanging against her bedroom door. Death amounted to too much of a crapshoot. She could be hit by a bus tomorrow, and she'd go to hell. Go directly to hell. Do not pass Go, do not collect two hundred dollars. But if she availed herself of the Fontaine method, she could be strapped with this baby. Two Ambien, a bottle of pinot gris, some leftover Halcion, and she'd be an unwed mother for eternity, wandering with no idea she was even dead.

She felt haunted, but from the inside this time.

Her phone rang. A private number.

"Mitz," a man said. Schlo. Her best work and her final job. He said, "I want you should see a picture tonight."

In the dark windows across the street, Mitzi watched her shadow self drain her glass of wine and pour another from the bottle on the windowsill. "It's after midnight."

"It's a midnight sneak preview," he said.

Mitzi told him, "We'll be late." She watched the shadows afloat in all the dim squares as others lifted glasses and tipped them to their lips. They were her Fontaine drinking buddies.

"Not too late," he said, "not for the scream part." He was downstairs, waiting for her.

Mitzi looked, and in place of the usual ambulance outside the front doors there was a limousine idling at the curb.

They'd been driving around aimlessly. Foster and the actress, they'd been hiding behind the murk of the car's heavily tinted windows, wondering how to buy food without getting recognized. The sun was setting. Maybe once it got fully dark.

A ways ahead a police cruiser was double-parked with an officer at the wheel. To avoid getting stuck behind it, or risk veering around it and drawing attention, Foster pulled to the curb. He shut off the engine and set the parking brake.

Blush asked to see the gun. Foster produced it from the pocket of his jacket, saying, "It's not loaded."

She reached across the front seat to take it, and he let her. She weighed it in her hand. "How'd you get this into Comic Con?"

Foster shrugged.

She leaned forward and lifted his phone off the dashboard. "If you got a gun in, it's because someone *wanted* you to get a gun in. Somebody wanted you to kidnap me." Her face deadpan, she mugged, "Probably my agent."

Foster considered his own theory about Lucinda guiding him. As if his daughter were somehow guiding his mission.

Blush unplugged his phone from the cigarette lighter. She reached to get one of his costume gloves off the seat, asking, "You mind?"

He didn't respond. He'd removed the heavy gloves the moment he'd climbed behind the wheel. They were spongy with sweat, as was the rest of his spandex costume.

Blush had long since peeled the damp executioner's hood off her head and flung it into the backseat. Apparently, she took his silence as consent and fitted a glove over one of her hands. With the other she held the phone as if to take a selfie. With the gloved hand she lifted the gun and pressed the muzzle hard against her cheek. Doing so, she twisted her face away and squeezed her eyes shut so tight that tears sprang from them and tracked black trails of mascara down her cheeks. Her downturned lips parted as if she were sobbing. The phone snapped a picture.

That's why she'd needed the glove. Cropped by the limits of a selfie, this would look like a man's hand shoving a gun into her movie star face as she recoiled in terror. The security cameras at the convention had caught him wearing these gloves. The pictures would be sent from his phone. Him, the fugitive from gun charges.

The phone chimed as she sent the photo. "This one's for the *New York Times*."

Blush swiped to a new screen that showed the current level of crowdfunded contributions toward her million-dollar ransom. "Fuck," she said, and not a happy *fuck*. Hers had clearly been an angry, disappointed *fuck*.

Foster pressed his case. "You played a babysitter who got stabbed." Then, as nonchalant as possible, "Who over-dubbed your scream?"

Her eyes narrowed, wary as if the question posed a threat. Her pretty face recovered its smug confidence. "I never use a scream double."

He followed her gaze to the police car parked up the block. He took his phone back and sourced a file. The shrill voice of a terrified girl shrieked.

The sound froze them both for a moment. It seemed to echo and hang in the air of the parked car.

Her arms folded across her chest, Blush swallowed. Flatly, she said, "That was me." Eyeing the police car, she slouched low.

Foster ventured, "It didn't sound like you."

"That's my job," she said. "I can sound like anyone."

Foster said, "Get out."

"It was *my scream*," Blush said. She grabbed the phone before he could play the recording a second time.

Foster hit the car's horn. It blared a long honk before he let up.

An old man on the sidewalk cupped his hand against her window and squinted to see inside. Crowds would attract the cops.

And Blush said, "Shit, okay. Okay?" She hid her face with her hands as more people peered into the car. "Maybe the scream wasn't me, okay?"

That's all Foster needed to hear.

The wine wasn't Ambien. It wasn't even Halcion, but it kept Mitzi in a nice holding pattern. The driver had doffed his cap as he opened the door of the limousine. Inside, Schlo had been waiting with chilled pinot gris and hot gossip. A stemmed glass of the former filled and waiting. Even as she stepped into the leather-padded interior and settled deep into the seats, she was reaching for the drink.

The car left the curb and glided along the empty nighttime streets with such a smoothness, such a liquid slide, that it seemed to her that the buildings and bus stops were moving while the limo sat in one place. As the producer pressed a button to close the partition between them and the driver, he asked, "You glad you're not Blush Gentry?"

Mitzi accepted the glass and brought it directly to her mouth. Giddy she felt. A little giddy after spending the last few days alone in her condo, like a dog that had been locked in the house for too long.

Without waiting, Schlo blurted, "Got herself kidnapped, poor kid."

He held up his phone, showing her a photo of the actress with a gun rammed cruelly against her forehead and tears washing mascara down her cheeks. He turned the phone to look at the picture. He shook his head with wonder. "After all those movies where she was eaten alive by rabid monkeys. Talk about karma."

The car nosed down a ramp, and they were gliding along the freeway.

Mitzi stopped drinking to catch her breath. With her half-empty glass she toasted, "Forget us our trespasses."

The producer reached the bottle from its bucket of ice on the bar. He leaned forward and poured her glass full.

The car nosed upward, following an exit ramp. It stopped at a light among tall, downtown buildings on an otherwise deserted street. Grates covered shop windows. Other drivers were few and far between.

The car slowed. Rolled to a stop. Or rather the world stopped scrolling past them, leaving only colors and flashes of light to flood the car windows. A neon-filled marquee.

They were parked in front of a theater. The Imperial. Above the theater's canopy a forest of dark minarets and spires rose against the nighttime sky. Dominating all of them, a looming concrete dome suggested the colossal size of the auditorium.

The Imperial stood alone among blocks of glass-walled towers. The last survivor of the downtown picture palaces built in the 1920s. The marquee lights spelled out "Midnight Sneak Preview," beyond the glass doors the lobby looked empty, just a stretch of red carpet and the gleam of polished brass and old gilded details. The box office was dark. A sign hung in the window read, "Sorry." The lack of empty parking spaces in every direction bore witness to how many hundreds of people must be inside. A thousand. Two thousand.

Squinting to see the lobby's arched ceiling and damask wallpaper, Mitzi whispered instead of talking aloud. "Does this have anything to do with Detroit?"

The producer patted the air as if to shush her. "Nothing happened in Detroit. Snow load is what happened in Detroit."

She put her glass to her lips and heard a soft ping. Like a small bell, as if someone had won something. It brought her attention to a dark spot on the blazing bright marquee. As she watched, another ping sounded. A bulb went dark. Another ping put out a third light. Bulbs bursting. The ringing rang together like a slot machine payout, like Christmas, as bulbs on every part of the canopy popped with machine-gun speed. So many so quickly, the name Imperial was illegible, and gone entirely in the next instant.

Something fell through Mitzi's field of vision, exploding on the sidewalk beside her window. Shards of it sprayed the car. Peering up, she could see the building's eaves where the red roof tiles rattled. Another tile broke loose and fell to shatter on the sidewalk.

A small pane in a large stained-glass window burst outward. Added to this, the popping lightbulbs and shattering clay tiles grew to a bright-sounding blizzard. A high-pitched fuselage of things breaking. The entire cluttered and complicated outline of the building seemed to shudder.

Against this ringing cacophony, the producer punched a number into his phone. "We have another incident," he told someone. His voice flat, grim with resignation. "Get the earthquake experts prepped with scenario number two." He spoke louder, raising his voice against the shrill din of windows bursting, exploding lightbulbs, and tiles. "Push our version out to the media now."

The lobby doors bulged outward and became a webbed haze of fractured safety glass. A concussive wave rocked the car. The tapered outline of each concrete minaret seemed to blur with vibration as a dull, grinding hum filled the night. A nearby car alarm wailed. A throbbing wail that echoed and reverberated in the canyon of high-rises.

* * *

Foster's car rocked from side to side. A breeze out of nowhere, it felt like, but more than a breeze. The car *listed* like a ship, pushed by a blast so strong it made the worn shock absorbers squeak. His body earthquake-trained, Foster sat upright, slamming his head against something. Against the steering wheel. He'd fallen asleep across the front seat. Adrenaline poisoned his blood.

From the backseat a voice asked, "You okay?" The words interrupted by a wail, an air-raid siren crescendo of wails. Car alarms by the hundreds. Blush rose on her elbows to peek out the rear window. Cars honked and trilled, their taillights and headlights flashing. Parked cars lining the empty dark streets.

Foster touched for blood where he'd hit his forehead and felt none. He saw Blush in the rearview mirror. She stared slack jawed at something in the distance. He looked in the same direction. There the skyline was changing shape. It called to mind the implosion of Las Vegas hotels. The controlled demolition of high-rise public housing projects. A thin tower sank into a cloud of dust. Other shapes alongside the tower also teetered and dropped out of sight. Strobes flashed as if from broken electrical cables.

A wine bottle flashed in Mitzi's memory. The way the bottle and her glass had exploded at the peak of someone's scream. Her elbow felt an echo of the pain as if her arm had its own memory. Even as she watched, the marquee canopy didn't fall so much as it seemed to melt in slow motion. It drooped until it lay in a tangle of steel and crushed neon tubing on the sidewalk. With the same slow wilting, a concrete spire dropped from the skyline. One minaret, then all of the minarets were dissolving into themselves. They sank into the bulk of the building as it fell dark. Moorish tiles, Mexican and Aztec-inspired ceramic tiles cracked and flaked off to reveal the poured-concrete shell of the theater. The lobby doors blocked by rubble, the scene screaming with alarms and approaching sirens, now only the great humped carcass of the auditorium roof stood against the dark sky.

For whatever reason, the driver kept them parked here at the curb, even as the columns and carved friezes of the building, the ornate chimneys and cupolas appeared to soften and droop and finally to drop out of sight. By itself, her hand brought the wineglass to her mouth. Her other hand sought the hard lump of a pill bottle in her jacket pocket.

The producer leaned next to her, holding his camera to the car window. Schlo filmed as the shivering mass of the structure, the great shattering, subsiding dome, began to slump, falling inward with a dull, dusty roar.

The facade toppled backward. The stained-glass windows and the statues in their mosaic-lined niches. Released from somewhere, a rooftop tank or cistern, a flood of water poured over the sinking wreckage. The water washed a tinkling wave of splintered glass and tile shards against the side of the limousine.

The great mass that had lined that side of the street, it continued to settle, shifting, sifting lower. The crumbling all of it disappeared below street level. The weight of rubble drove downward into whatever basement or sub-basements had been beneath the structure. So deep Mitzi could see ruptured water mains spouting into the void from several locations.

The pulverized concrete and the remnants of red plush sank lower as the dark waters rose higher and closed over them. And in short order the spouting water mains themselves were submerged, and the entire site was transformed into a fairly large, very square lake.

A calm lake of black water. As dark and ominous as the La Brea tar pits. Nothing save a scattering of popcorn floated on this still, silent surface.

A building was being demolished. Foster seized on the idea. That would explain the mob of cars parking downtown so late: spectators. The demolition was taking place at this predawn hour for safety reasons. This, he told himself, made total sense.

Blush said, "Turn on the radio." Sirens grew louder. "Turn on the radio, and get us out of here." Her voice flat with demand.

In this world of streaming everything, a radio seemed as archaic as a telegram. Foster had to find the ignition with the key and turn it a notch before he could work the radio knobs. Flashing emergency lights were approaching, lashing the scene with blue and red.

Blush cowered in the backseat. "Drive!" She was slipping the battery into her phone.

"It was a tremor." Foster craned his neck to check for traffic on the empty street and pulled away from the curb. The only other car in motion was a limousine passing them, headed off in the opposite direction, accelerating fast.

Blush gazed out the rear window. "Get us on the freeway. Hurry." She threw both arms over the back of the front seat. Phone in hand, she held it for him to see the screen. A tinny shriek sounded from the phone's speakers. The car radio announced, "...suspected microquake..."

Blush snarled at the radio, "Microquake?"

Foster risked a glance at the screen.

On the phone some cheesy disaster movie played. Countless screaming teenagers filled a theater, row upon row of contorted faces. Boys and girls, standing upon or sitting in red velvet seats. Their hands held up, fingers splayed as chunks of golden concrete crashed down upon them. The camera's perspective swung upward to show an ornate frescoed ceiling framed in cornices of gesso and stucco, all of this architecture cracking to pieces and thundering down. The painted clouds and angels plunged from a concrete sky. And in the center of this a stupendous chandelier of what appeared to be bronze, blazing with a forest of electric candles and dripping with swags and fobs of faceted crystal. This behemoth blinked, went dark, swayed a moment and dropped. The camera shot followed its plunge, short and fast. It thudded with the impact of a meteor striking the earth, crushing to instant silence the teenage and tweenage throngs. The crash sent up geysers of sparks.

Foster snorted, annoyed. Nervous. Not sure why she was showing him this camp disaster flick. His forehead still throbbed from where he'd conked it on the steering wheel. The pain his only guarantee this wasn't a nightmare.

This disaster movie, it appeared to take place within a movie palace. In the distance a screen showed an actor, his tortured face twisted in pain, his enormous mouth screaming. It was his scream that the audience seemed to be mimicking. As if the massed crowd was reacting in complete sympathy, screaming in the same pitch as his scream as the building around them shook to pieces and collapsed upon them.

The camera's perspective was moving now, shifting sideways as an adjacent wall gave way, burying victims beneath a landslide of red velvet wallpaper and concrete. Steel rebar twisted like licorice. Other arms, other people in the background held phones as if documenting their own last moments. This cascade of statuary and columns continued to flatten phone-waving hordes, killing them instantly until the scene shown on Blush's phone went dark and silent. Silent and dead, the screen reflecting only the dim shadows of Foster's face.

It took Mitzi a moment to recognize herself. She'd been in the studio, scream surfing through the inventory. Combing through the decades of tapes in the hope she might find the original of the orchiectomy scream. What she'd do with it she had no idea.

She'd chosen a tape at random. Hit Play. And there she was, some lost version of herself. Hardly recognizable, even to her. The words woozy and strung out, the voice on the tape asked, "Do you know what the Wilhelm scream is, dear?"

Audible on the tape, a stomach growled. "Sorry," a girl, some mystery girl, mumbled. "All this food talk makes me hungry."

Her words slurred on the tape, Mitzi said, "Not to worry. You won't be hungry much longer."

She and the girl continued to talk. The quality of their voices improved as the microphones seemed to be adjusted and the levels on the board were checked and rechecked.

The girl mumbled, "English muffins...biscuits and gravy..."

Mitzi was only half listening to the tape when the scream exploded, a burst of agony from every speaker in the studio.

At its peak the shriek broke apart into short, jagged

cries, each more quiet, ebbing, ending in ragged breathing, each gasp shorter, trailing off with a final long exhale.

A rasp and click sounded on the tape. A sound Mitzi knew from every headache of her life. The sound of a cigarette lighter sparking. The sizzle of a cigarette being lit. The draw of a long inhale and the crackle of tobacco burning, a sound so true-to-life that even now she sniffed the air for smoke. A recording so clear and pure that it seemed to trump the fact that she was alone. She sat alone at the console in a locked studio, listening to sounds so real that they might be ghosts in the room, unseen. Or that she, herself, might be the ghost listening to a world without her.

Footsteps approached on the tape and a voice called out, "Gentlemen!" This new voice belonged to a man. The sensible, practical voice of Dr. Adamah, a devout smoker. How long he'd also been in that room, there was no telling.

Mitzi closed her eyes to hear better. In the dark, the past took over the room.

The doctor called out, "Gentlemen, you may clean up the scene now."

Blush asked for a lug wrench. "Like for changing tires? Do you have one?" she clarified. They'd parked at a wide spot in the road, both of them sitting in the front seat by now.

Foster couldn't say if he had, not for certain, so he walked around to open the trunk.

They'd followed a narrow street up into the nighttime hills, rising above the city. At her direction, he'd turned onto a dark lane. His headlights had washed over a sign that read Private Drive as the surrounding houses had fallen away behind them. Their path had traced the thin spine of a high ridge with one side falling away in a steep, rutted slope. From this height he could see downtown, where helicopters circled playing searchlights over a space between buildings. Sirens wailed.

Dogs, dogs and coyotes alike, every canine in the greater Los Angeles Basin howled along with those sirens. An eerie reminder of how every animal was still wild.

The night air smelled of juniper and sage. In the trunk Foster felt around in the dark until he produced a steel bar bent at an angle. One end was cast into a hexagonal socket to fit lug nuts. The opposite end was pinched into a sharp wedge for prying off hubcaps and wheel covers.

Blush stood next to him now and took the tool out of his hands. Striding away, she held the lug wrench in one fist and swung it like a weapon to slap the palm of her opposite hand. Foster hurried to catch up as she followed a stucco wall that lined the side of the road opposite the view. Pink stucco, flaking and crumbling, too high to see over. Every few steps signs for a security service were fixed to the wall. As were No Trespassing signs, screwed to the wall and bleeding trails of rust stains. Ahead, the chimneys and rooflines of a dark house rose above the ragged top of the wall.

Near the house, they came to a gateway. Pure movie studio Spanish Renaissance, the gates were, with twisted ironwork branching and crisscrossed. Iron birds roosted among the bars. Through these they walked up a circular driveway to large doors barricaded with plywood. The unpainted sheet of wood, buckled and warped, clung to the house like a scab. Stapled there, a sun-bleached sign warned them "No Trespassing by Writ of Foreclosure." With surprising violence, Blush reared back and lunged, stabbing the sharp end of the lug wrench under one edge of the wood. She worked the bar up and down to sink it deeper, then yanked at the wood. The plywood splintered around the screws that held it.

Foster stepped close and put his hands around the bar. They pulled together, and the plywood crackled like bones breaking in the movies. Not a loud noise, but a lot of noise on a night so quiet and a street so deserted. It broke away along three edges and swung aside. Beneath it, a door showed hazy with spiderwebs.

Blush dug into her coat pocket to bring forth a ring of keys. One she fit into the deadbolt and turned. A second key she put into the knob.

The door stuck along the bottom, opening inward, rubbing against the threshold with a barking rasp. She snaked a hand inside the frame.

Foster heard the click-click of a switch, but no lights came on.

"Give me your hand," she said.

The light from the street filtered inside only a few steps. The air wafting out smelled hot, a musty heat built up over months of day-to-day sun not relieved by open windows at night or air-conditioning. Into that stale smell Blush stepped. Past that point, she dragged him as she took long, confident strides into the dark.

Mitzi had been washing dishes. Mostly wineglasses. Her hands had held the glass wrong, a too-strong grip on a too-slippery soapy-smooth glass with the results one might expect. The little outcry glass makes, and the glass failing, surrendering itself to become two pieces. Each with one razor-sharp edge.

She'd been so tense. The tape recording playing and repeating in her mind. Dr. Adamah's words looped in her memory, as did those of the dying girl. A waitress? In addition the troubling voices of men she'd never met but who seemed to know her. Worst was her own mysterious other self, that slurred voice, a drooling drunk, but undeniably her. The Village Idiot voice of Mitzi Ives. Tension clenched her teeth. No muscle could relax as she considered the mystery. It was then the glass broke.

Before she'd felt anything, the sudsy water in the sink turned dark red. Proof of how a deep slice in warm water might not hurt, not at first. She brought her hand to the surface, and the skin below her thumb, below the ham of her thumb, spouted like a red whale. The slice curved like the bite from a child's mouth. It surged with blood Mitzi couldn't bear to look at, so she plunged the hand back to the bottom of the sink.

Warm water and a cut so deep, her body was filling the sink as if she were plumbing.

She wondered how long the decision to survive was hers to make. If she ought to call someone to come rescue her. Or to simply wait for her body to make the other choice.

Foster let himself be dragged along. His free hand brushed smooth metal and the rough cages he took to be the burners of a gas stove. His leg slid along the metal door of a refrigerator, jarring his hip bone against the handle. Flailing in the dark, his free hand felt the knobs and edges of cabinet doors and drawer fronts. He didn't lift his feet for fear of tripping over something, and the floor felt like smooth tile under his shuffling.

Now all he knew of Blush Gentry was her smell and the feel of her strong, smooth hand. He could guess at the size of rooms. To judge by the echoes the spaces must've been huge.

Blush stopped. "Take the handrail to your right," she said. "We're going up a flight of stairs."

Foster waved blindly until he found the rail. A dimly lit archway rose above them. At the top of the steps, they entered a room large enough to host a basketball game. The first blue shade of morning filtered through the dirty windows. Dust cushioned their steps.

"Your house?" he asked. He was whispering. A house without food or water. A house without heat or power, it didn't seem such a great hideout. He followed her to a built-in bookcase where she shoved aside some leather-bound volumes.

Her fingers worked at something in the shadows at the back of a shelf. A pneumatic hiss sounded, and the bookcase swung away from them, revealing a dark space behind it.

Blush touched the wall within and lights blazed. She touched again, a keypad mounted there, and cool air issued from vents near the ceiling. She waved him inside, saying, "Panic room. Earthquake preparation. Bottled water. Generator." She plucked her phone from her bag. "No cell phone reception because the place is lead-lined or zinc-lined or something in the event of a nuclear bomb…" She pointed toward an old-school phone mounted on one wall and trailing a long, coiled cord. "But we do have a landline. Unlisted, of course."

Right on cue, the phone rang.

Blush stared at it, her face dark with worry. It rang seven times and stopped. She sighed, "Wrong number."

The ringing began again. Seven rings, then it stopped. As it began again, she reached to lift the receiver and bring it to her ear. "Schlo!" She cupped a hand to cover the mouthpiece and whispered to Foster, "He's a friend. A producer, but a good guy." Into the receiver she said, "Let me put you on speakerphone."

The voice burst into the room like an extended belch. "I knew where to find you," it said. "You there with your kidnapper?"

"Foster." Blush nodded to indicate the phone, the little mesh-covered speaker on it. "This is Schlo. Schlo produced the babysitter bloodbath."

The belch said, "Blush, little girl. You're not planning to attend the Oscars, are you?"

Blush cast another worried look at Foster. "That was my plan," she said.

The belch insisted, "Just don't. Trust me." The connection went dead.

Blush dropped her bag and shucked her jacket before ducking away. To retrieve the lug wrench. To camouflage the damage they'd done to the plywood covering the street door. As she left she swung the bookcase shut behind her.

With no idea how to open it, Foster became the captive.

He dug the phone from his pocket and snapped the battery into place. So what if he couldn't get a signal? The police couldn't find his location, either. He swiped through screens. He wanted to show this movie star something. A video. So what if it was grainy and without sound? It lasted no longer than a birthday candle, but it was the most important movie in his life.

Schlo proved himself to be no mere friend. Such a prince, he bribed the doorman of the Fontaine. That was Schlo.

The doorman used a passkey and they found Mitzi insensate, the pile of her blacked out next to the kitchen sink, redecorating the cork tile to blood red. How he knew to do this, who knows. But Schlo sent the doorman out for superglue and hydrogen peroxide, and Schlo got Mitzi's arm above her heart and applied pressure. He could've been a doctor.

Levelheaded like a person wouldn't believe, he said, "Mitz, what I don't know could fill Yankee Stadium, but I do know something's wrong."

The Imperial, the falling down of it. A palace of a landmark building that had withstood its share of earthquakes, the government was calling it an earthquake. Detroit they were calling snow load. The next theater, God forbid, they'd call it terrorism.

Mitzi should pack her bags is what the man meant. Take the money she'd socked away and pull a Roman Polanski. "Destroy the master tape," he ordered her. "This isn't only me talking. It's our entire industry. We've been duped."

Schlo was like a wizard. Maybe she wasn't the first girl he'd glued the cuts in her wrist shut, but Schlo rinsed the area with ice and dusted it with cream of tartar. And when the bleeding stopped for just a moment, he pinched the cut closed and dripped on superglue.

Hollywood being Hollywood, who didn't want to play the hero?

Woozy on the kitchen floor, she asked, "But what's happening?"

Standing over her, Schlo said, "It's Jericho! Baby girl, Jericho is what's happening."

Foster showed her the video last. First they got loaded, a little loaded but for a long time, on the bottle of rum she brought back after fixing the street door so it wouldn't attract attention. Rum because she liked the sweetness, like high school parties she'd never attended because she'd been too busy playing the role of a teenage slattern to actually slattern around. Playing a sexpot had kept her a virgin until her first marriage.

They were camped out in her panic room. Blush lifted her glass and made a grand sweep. "How do you think I could *almost afford* this wonderful house?"

Even to judge from what little he'd seen, the place was massive.

"Sure," she said with chagrin, "it's big for a house, but small for a world." When she'd bought it at the height of her career, she'd been just as trapped in it as she was now. Photographers waited outside to follow her. Lunatic fans waited.

They'd poured more rum. More Coke. They toasted her crowdfunding when it broke twenty grand.

They'd fallen silent. Still sipping their drinks as the television showed a live on-location report of the first human remains being recovered from the Imperial Theater. Body bag after bag, each holding something too small to be a whole person. Not even a teenager.

She'd fallen asleep, and Gates Foster had told her sleeping self about the wreck of Lucinda's fake funeral and how a fellow member of the support group, a doctor even, had botched the Bible reading. Instead of reading the section Foster had chosen, the man had read from the book of Joshua. The account of Joshua's army shouting until their combined voices had collapsed the walls of a city.

He told her sleeping form how the funeral itself had evolved so quickly into a public humiliation. Almost as if it had been an organized conspiracy to goad him into rage.

On television the newscast broke to show Amber making an emotional plea for him to free his hostage and turn himself in to the police. Poor Amber.

Blinking awake from her nap, Blush said, "Don't even think about it, buster." She looked at the woman on-screen, Foster's ex-wife, and said, "She's pretty. Did your little girl take after her?"

Only then did Foster show her the gallery on his phone. First his favorite photos of Lucinda, then various age-progressed portraits that had appeared on milk cartons over the past seventeen years. With each one, yes, she did look more like her mother.

He showed her his rogue's gallery of pedophiles and described his endless hunt. As if he were tracking down Nazi war criminals. The irony being that now he was the one hunted.

Only after all of that did Foster show her the video. The soundless few seconds. The grainy security video lasting no longer than a birthday candle, it showed Lucinda being led down a hallway and out a door of the Parker-Morris Building. She was holding hands with a slightly older girl. Most likely around twelve, the girl stood a head taller as she led the smaller girl through the door to the street and out of sight forever.

"Lucy had always wanted a sibling," he said as Blush played and replayed the short video captured by a security camera so long ago. "She'd always ask us to have another baby so she could have an older sister," he remembered, "but we tried to explain that the older one had to come *before*."

Blush paused the video at the moment the older girl's face seemed most visible. "I wonder what she looks like now." Her eyes squinted to study the coarse image.

Foster took back the phone. He swiped through a gallery of images. "I asked the same people who did the age progression..." He handed the phone back, saying, "Of course, I had to pay for it myself."

There on the screen was a woman in her late twenties, possibly thirty years old. Clearly the unknown girl from the video, but her blonde hair had grown a shade darker. Her round face had thinned, giving her wide cheekbones and accentuating her eyes. She was lovely, the kidnapper. It felt wrong to call a twelve-year-old a kidnapper. It felt wrong to think of himself as a kidnapper. If anything, this was a mutual kidnapping.

Blush looked at the photo of the grown girl. She looked

a long time, long enough for Foster to finish his drink and reach for the bottle.

As he offered to fill her glass, she said, "I know her."

The knife wouldn't fit in Mitzi's handbag. The blade was too long: a German Lauffer Carvingware knife. From where she couldn't venture a guess, but she'd found it in the studio prop room still wrapped in FedEx packaging.

Her damaged wrist she'd wrapped in paper towels, where it was still glued. Stitches or staples or whatever doctors did these days, she still needed doing.

But who should Mitzi Ives meet at the doctor's office but a moving van. A crew of men in blue uniforms, they were carting sealed boxes out the front door of the office.

Taped in the front window of the building was a sign that read "This Space for Lease."

While down the block sat the doctor's Daimler with the good leather seats, a Boston fern inside. This Boston fern that used to look so small on a plant stand in the only window of the waiting room, in the doctor's car it filled the whole backseat.

Mitzi didn't panic. She made polite, nodding eye contact with the movers. She edged past them through the street door and into the empty waiting room.

If the movers noticed or not, she held up the FedEx package as if she were just delivering it. The doctor stepped out of his examining room. Just pulling on his coat. Just this close to a clean getaway, he saw Mitzi and smirked.

He snapped his fingers until one moving man looked. "That"—the doctor indicated the Toledo scale—"goes to the warehouse, also."

The scale the man struggled to lift. He carted it to the door, and for just that long Mitzi saw her chance. She fumbled the knife out of its wrapping and waved it toward the examining room.

The doctor rolled his eyes. Shook his head at Mitzi's knife wielding, but walked back.

The place, a person wouldn't know it. Stripped. Even the sink, gone. Just the plumbing for the water and the drain stubbed off at the wall. Already some workman had come through with a putty knife and prepped for new paint. The doctor, he waved Mitzi inside and closed the door. Locked it. Locked himself inside with a knife wielder. He said, "You won't stab me, Mitzi." He looked at the paper towels wrapped so tightly. Asking, like he cared, he asked, "What's up with your hand?"

Mitzi brought the knife up a little, asking, "Who are you to say I won't stab you?"

"Because," Adamah said, "you're a coward." He stepped closer and reached for the wounded wrist. "You're the worst kind of victim: a victim who thinks she's a villain."

Mitzi let him take the wrist and begin stripping away the paper towels.

As he did so, the doctor said, "It's sickening the way you come running to me for absolution." He uncovered the cut, the slash still puckered shut under a shining layer of glue. "Look what you've done," he said, touching the wound tenderly. "You stupid piece of shit." Softly he said this. "You couldn't even cut yourself adequately."

With the doctor so close, leaning low to see the damage, Mitzi, she brought up the knife. Laid it against Adamah's throat. Held the honed edge of it to his throat. "You don't know anything," said Mitzi. "I've murdered dozens of people in ways you'd never imagine."

Not pulling away, even leaning his neck against the blade, the doctor told her, "Prove me wrong." He tossed his head to indicate the waiting room, the movers. "They won't know. They'll be gone in a moment. Kill me."

Afraid, Mitzi pulled back the knife, but the doctor leaned closer until his throat was creased by the blade, again. Mitzi pulled it away and held it at arm's length. Unnerved, she said, "Not until I get some answers."

The doctor slipped a hand into his coat pocket. A plastic box marked First Aid he took out. A needle pre-threaded with a length of nylon string he took out of that. A sealed plastic packet like of ketchup, he tore in half and pulled out a gauze smelling like rubbing alcohol.

"Give me your hand," he ordered. As he'd done since Mitzi was a teenager, he took Mitzi around one wrist and shook it and told her, "Hold still, please!" And this alcohol swab he began swabbing across the patch of glue, the smell of which brought tears to Mitzi's eyes and almost made her drop the knife because it stung so much, the swabbing did.

She was a butcher. Mitzi knew it. A Last Wave Feminist. A serial butcher and a killer, and nobody was going to say she wasn't.

The doctor held the damaged hand firmly, teasing her, "Look at you. Your stomach is so weak you can't bear to watch someone eat a runny egg." A sham, the office had been. For so many years, set dressing.

The needle entered her skin, and the doctor asked, "Remember I told you how a siren makes dogs howl?" The needle exited, pulling a few seconds of string through her hand. "A siren triggers a pack instinct in all dogs," continued the doctor. "It's a primal scream dogs must share in."

As Mitzi kept her eyes on the wall, the needle entered again. It exited, tugging the string through her skin.

The doctor said, "Imagine if there was some human equivalent. A cry like Walt Whitman's *barbaric yawp* that would evoke the primal scream of everyone who heard it." The needle entered. Exited. String moved under the skin.

Mitzi winced. As the string pulled, she felt herself pulled. A puppet, she felt like, tethered to the doctor's words. As if she were a kite or a balloon, something with which the doctor played. Under the smell of cigarettes, the smell of bleach on his skin. The smell of her father she'd swallowed so many pills to forget.

"Your father was a great man," said the doctor. The needle entering. Exiting. That tugging at something inside

Mitzi. "Your father was the last in a long chain of men on this magnificent project."

The needle pricked into her skin, drove through and emerged dragging the string behind it. "My advice to you is this," said Adamah. "Take your baby and your money. People are going to call upon you. Give them the master of the last scream. Take your baby and your money and begin a new life someplace beautiful."

Afraid to move, leashed by that strand of nylon, Mitzi couldn't pull away. The pain, the sting felt small, but it was the fear of so much thread laced through her and how it would tear open, rip open like a zipper, if she tried to escape.

"You've done nothing." The doctor said the words with contempt. "Nothing messy. Oh, you knew how to control the recording levels and the brightness. You worked that magic. It wasn't as if we could bring in an outsider." The string tugged, stretching the skin. "But you never killed anyone."

Mitzi managed, "But I did." Sweat pasted the blouse to her back and rolled down the inner sides of her arms.

The doctor leaned so close his breath was warm against the wounded hand. He cinched a knot and used his teeth to bite off the extra thread. He said, "No. I killed them. You were too squeamish, not a bit like your father."

Mitzi turned to examine her hand. The neat row of stitches that now closed the wound.

* * *

As Blush told it, first the PayDay candy bars had disappeared. No one would say where to. It wasn't as if the vending machines had run out and someone had forgotten to restock. The next day the Snickers were all gone, the spiral of metal that held the Snickers was just some empty spring. Gone in quick succession were the peanut butter cups, then those cellophane packages holding orange crackers sandwiched around peanut butter in the middle.

The vending machines were all but barren save for some old Red Vines and packets of cherry Life Savers nobody wanted. Some fossilized Skittles.

Blush Gentry told her story from a beanbag chair. She and Foster, sealed inside the panic room. Without a window, with the air recirculation system blasting, neither could tell if it was day or night. Their drinking had given way to storytelling.

It was into this unforgiving peanut-free world that she had gone each day. And in exchange for every treat they'd loved and lost, the still peanut shell-shocked students of the sixth grade got a new classmate by the name of Lawton Taylor Koestler.

Blush pulled a who-cares? face. "He was a regular kid. Nothing two-headed about him."

The only thing not to like was the kid's mother, Mrs. Koestler, who accompanied her son to class on his first day and asked to speak to the kids in his grade. The teacher asked Lawton to step into the hall.

Her son was a very sick boy, Mrs. Koestler told Blush and her classmates. Deathly allergic to almost everything. But peanuts especially. And it was the responsibility of every boy and girl to ensure that Lawton never be exposed to peanuts in any form or, for that matter, any food that had been processed or packaged in any facility that dealt with peanuts. And she described, this Mrs. Koestler, how the tiniest particle of peanut enzyme would spur a full-body immune system reaction. Lawton's lungs would quit working. His tongue would swell to suffocate him.

"There was no Mr. Koestler," Blush said. "No wonder. The woman was a harpy."

Blush pulled a handful of her hair near her face and began to pick through the strands, frowning when she found a gray one. "He made a basket from center court once, three points, and that alone should've made him popular, but his mom was a disability no kid could've got past."

At times she'd stop mid-story. She'd get up and go to the touchpad and shut off the air. In the absence of the humming fans and blowers she'd listen as if she'd heard someone enter the house. They were walled in. Safe from nuclear attack, and she was nervous about a burglar. During these tense silences the air would grow warm and damp with their breathing.

After a spell of listening, listening and thinking, she'd activate the air-conditioning and settle back in her bean-bag chair. At these pauses she seemed to be debating how far to tell this story.

She asked, "Have you heard of Munchausen syndrome?"

Foster nodded. "A person tells fantastic lies. Usually about his health, right?"

She smiled at a memory. "He came to our house for dinner one time. Did not eat a bite. I could tell he was terrified of the food. My mom felt sorry for him."

The problem, her father told her, wasn't just peanuts. It could be wasps. Bee stings. A friend of his had been riding a motorcycle and caught a bee in the face. He'd never been allergic, but now his cheeks had begun to swell. The guy's vision blurred, and his throat swelled shut. All while still zooming along at freeway speeds. This friend of her father, he'd steered for the shoulder and braked hard, and even then he saw his own death, saw the real world disappearing and felt the motorcycle skid and topple onto the gravel. Blind and suffocating, he fell. A terrible pain shot up his leg, yet he didn't die.

As doctors explained it, Blush's father said, the cycle's hot tailpipe had burned the man's leg. Burned it to the bone. And the subsequent rush of natural adrenaline had stopped the allergic reaction. For the rest of his life, the man walked with a limp, but at least he had a life.

It had been her father who'd suggested Munchausen's by proxy. Blush and her father had been washing dishes after the meal. After Lawton Koestler had gone home hungry. Munchausen's by proxy was a mental illness and a form of child abuse. It prompted a parent to convince a child that he was frail. That he was allergic to everything or had a debilitating disease. It had been a lot for her eleven-year-old brain to grapple with.

"I thought I could cure him," said Blush.

She rolled onto her side, scrunching the beanbag, so she could look straight at Foster. "I haven't always been eaten alive by creatures from outer space, you know. I was raised in Idaho." She nodded as if to assure him she wasn't lying. "Mountains. Geodes."

As a kid she'd been hiking and camping every free moment. "I didn't grow up wanting to be hacked to pieces by an axe murderer." She'd wanted to be a gemologist.

Foster laughed. "Really? A gemologist?"

"Don't laugh," she laughed. "Idaho is called the Gem State."

Still laughing, he said, "Sorry, I'm sure you'd make a great..." He couldn't say it with a straight face.

She said, "I knew schist and basalt and talus slopes." She was a scientist at heart. So she talked Lawton into going on a hike one Saturday, just the two of them. She packed her own lunch. His mother packed him something nut-free and gluten-free, something non-soy and lactose-free. "And we took off on the trail to the top of Beech Mountain."

She looked at Foster without speaking. The moment stretched as if she were testing him. This was a trial to see if he'd interrupt and change the subject, or if Foster was actually listening and engaged in her story. He allowed the minutes of silence to pass.

She said, "Don't laugh, but I used to know every bird on sight. I knew their songs, too."

Foster didn't laugh.

"I was such a Disney princess, too." She rolled her eyes at the memory. "The way Prince Charming woke Sleeping Beauty with a kiss, that's how I planned to rescue Lawton Koestler."

She'd eaten a peanut, a handful of Spanish peanuts, at breakfast. When they arrived at the peak of Beech Mountain, she'd caught him around the waist and kissed him on the mouth. She'd felt his body go stiff, but the longer she kissed him the more he relaxed, until he was kissing her back. The kiss lasted until they had to step away from each other and gasp for air. Forests and meadows rolled off in every direction. Eagles circled below them, they were so high in the mountains.

"It turned out like the other story—the Snow White story—especially the part where the witch makes Snow White bite the poison apple." Her kiss had been nice. A nice kiss. They'd kissed a second time, and his mouth had a milk taste, like boys who are good at sports taste. She didn't say anything, not right away, but she was thrilled. She hadn't cured him, but she'd proved he wasn't sick to begin with.

She'd planned to tell him he wasn't sick as soon as they got home. He wasn't weak. He only had a crazy mother is all.

Again Blush Gentry waited in silence. Testing Foster's

attention. Maybe wishing he'd interrupt and redirect the conversation to the theater collapse, the crowdfunding, something safe.

When he did not, she continued, "We hadn't come down the trail a few steps before he started to wheeze…"

He had a pen, a kind of needle he carried in order to inject himself if he had such a reaction. But it was late October with no bees around and certainly no peanuts to worry about, and he'd left the injection pen in his jacket in Blush's family car when they'd been dropped off. On a day this warm, he didn't figure to need a jacket.

Events unfolded pretty much the way his mother had predicted. His face turned meat red and the skin swelled around his eyes and mouth. He looked like a stranger who couldn't breathe, clawing off his shirt and clawing at his skinny red chest and arms.

She tried to cover him up, to keep him warm, but more embarrassed by his nakedness and distress. As if she could hide the damage she'd done simply by keeping his clothes on him. When she'd suggested running down to get help, he'd grabbed her hand and begged. The trailhead was miles, hours away, and there was no guarantee her father would already be waiting.

"He asked me not to leave him," she said. Lawton thought he was going to die. His breathing was a whistle through the raw swelling inside his throat. He knew he was going to die, and he didn't want to die alone.

She helped him stretch out on the pine needles and

hoped that position would help. It would be like an epileptic seizure, she hoped, and he'd return to normal after a bit. But his eyes began to swell shut and his mouth gaped wider as he tried to draw the next breath. His chest heaved, held the air, and blew it out with a cry, each exhale erupting with specks of blood from his burning throat.

Sunk in her beanbag chair, Blush waited now in silence as if asking Foster's permission to complete the horror. No longer was she telling a sweet story to entertain him and explain herself. Now she'd be sharing a burden that he'd struggle to carry for the rest of his life. She'd inflicted something and waited to hear his acceptance or rejection of it.

"Lawton's eyes were swollen shut, but he raised an arm and whispered, 'Dad.'" His swollen purple lips had twisted into a smile, and he'd tried to sit upright even as Blush pushed to hold him flat on the ground.

"It's my dad!" he insisted, gasping. "He's here to rescue me!"

Some words, Foster wished he could see coming. *Dad*, for instance, left him gut-shot. His belly couldn't hurt more if someone had designed this story to torture him.

The eleven-year-old Blush saw nothing. The trail stretched empty in both directions. They wouldn't have daylight for much longer, but she couldn't bear to leave him to die in the dark. A blinded sixth grader facing death by himself in a dark forest.

It didn't occur to her that she might soon be a sixth-grade

murderer alone with the dead body of her victim in those woods at night.

That's when her father's words came back to her. About the motorcycle and the bee sting. Little Blush, she fumbled a book of matches out of her backpack. She slipped off one of Lawton's shoes and socks and rolled up the pant leg to expose the skin where a scar wouldn't show for the rest of his life. She was so sure she could save him. Instead of being a Disney princess, now she was someone out of Hans Christian Andersen. The Little Match Girl. And instead of bringing comfort, when she lit each match and held the flame to Lawton's leg, he screamed.

Foster slugged back his drink and helped himself to another.

Instead of saving Lawton, each match brought the stink of sulfur and scorching flesh. The skin of his ankle blistered and split. Split and hissed. Hissed and sizzled.

Desperate, she lit the whole pack and tortured him until the flames sputtered and left them in total darkness: The Little Match Girl and her victim.

In lieu of saving Lawton Koestler more, Blush Gentry sat beside him and held his hand. "My dogs," he raved hoarsely. "Oh Dad, oh Daddy!" Nothing approached. Only the wind rose in the trees as the daylight faded. Leaves were sifting down to half bury them in a layer of dirty yellow.

Lawton Koestler calmed. His wheezing breath slowed. He asked, "Can't you see them?"

Blush could see nothing. The night settles fast in the mountains, and she might die as surely as Lawton was dying if she stayed too long in the open as temperatures fell.

In the panic room, her words broke and she swallowed them and went quiet for long stretches. From this point she spoke as if it didn't matter whether or not Foster was listening.

"He told me that his father had died from the same allergy," she said. And that Mr. Koestler had come to meet his son and escort his son to the next life. Likewise, dogs were present. Family dogs that had died when Lawton was barely walking, but they, too, had come to guide him and give him comfort.

In Foster's mind flashed the mysterious girl in the security video, who seemed to be leading his Lucinda away to safety, but in all likelihood to her doom.

All this time the young Blush Gentry, that wannabe gemologist, she had held Lawton's hand, even as it grew colder and his breathing grew fainter. She wanted to confess about the kiss, about eating peanuts before the kiss, and about Prince Charming rescuing Sleeping Beauty, but she couldn't interrupt his talking about dogs she couldn't see or a father who wasn't there. His hand around hers hardened into a manacle, and he was too heavy to budge. She was a girl who knew how the wind in the trees all night could sound like someone coming to the rescue. And how, at the same time, it could sound like a mountain lion coming in for the kill.

Defeated by her own story, Blush said, "That's why I allow alligators to tear me apart, naked." And reached for her own glass of rum and Coke.

Mitzi reached for the gold cuff links set with rubies.

Schlo told her, "Not those. God forbid." He said, "I want my son should have those." He held a martini and sloshed it to indicate a pair set with green stones. "If you please, I'll wear the malachite."

The cuff links, as well as various tie tacks and tie bars, not to mention the extra studs to his tux shirt and the flower for his lapel, were displayed on a velvet-lined tray atop the bureau in his bedroom. As she reached for the malachite ones, Mitzi caught sight of herself in the bureau's mirror.

With a finger pointed at the tray, Schlo said, "Not the Piaget, either. I'll wear the Timex, just in case."

There in the mirror was a woman in her late twenties, possibly thirty years old. Her blonde hair was growing a shade darker. Her round face had thinned, giving her wide cheekbones and accentuating her eyes. She was getting her looks back. Pregnancy would do that. She asked, "Do I look like a killer?"

In the mirror, Schlo shot her a look. "Don't brood," he said. "You who couldn't kill a fly?" He tugged back the sleeve of his jacket and offered a hand.

She folded back the French cuff of his shirt and matched the holes. Slipped the cuff link into place and opened the toggle. She reached for the other cuff.

He looked at her as if gauging whether this was a story or a confession. And was this something he wanted to hear? He grinned. "Don't make me laugh or I'll sweat." He shifted his bulky torso inside the tuxedo jacket.

She worked the second cuff link into place. This she could remember doing for her father on special nights like tonight. The Academy Awards ceremony, such a night. And one time she'd actually gone with him, her father, but not a second time. Never again. Not after everyone seated around them had risen and left the auditorium. Their neighbors had decamped to watch events from the lounge, on the television screens in the bar. And when the place-holders, those dressed-up aspiring actors had filled the empty seats, when even those camera-ready nobodies had stood awkwardly and slinked away, then Mitzi Ives had felt shame as only a child can suffer shame. She'd known the television cameras would never swing her way, not and risk revealing a small field of empty seats in the audience otherwise packed with Hollywood luminaries.

No, Mitzi had never again begged her father to take her. But his cuff links she'd done, and his bow tie she'd learned to tie. And tonight the same she was doing for Schlo.

The bedroom television showed the crowds currently outside the Dolby Theatre. The tiered seating that lined the red carpet, and the camera crews stationed at intervals to interview the arriving guests.

"Your father," Schlo said, glowering at his reflection in the mirror, "him I could see as a killer."

Mitzi flipped up the tabs on his shirt collar and looped the tie around his neck. She crossed the two ends under his chin and tried to balance the loops.

The scream movie had been nominated for Best Sound. Not nominated due to being something good, but nominated due to politics and how the industry needed to prove they hadn't launched a horror flick that had already smashed dead with concrete almost three thousand teenagers if you combined the Imperial with what had happened in Detroit. Call it snow load or a tiny, one-city-block-sized earthquake, the reporters were reporting whatever the people who owned the news told them to report.

Not every screening had ended in disaster. Plenty of showings in other venues had been uneventful, but two was pattern enough to scare most people away from theaters.

Tonight, all of Tinseltown was turning out, conscripted as human guinea pigs. In one big act of faith, they'd watch the scream segment together, all the stars attired in their loaned designer finery and jewels. Just to prove to the world that moviegoing was safe.

Still, Schlo's wife, she complained she had a backache just to stay home. And Schlo, he wasn't wearing the ruby cuff links. Or the Piaget. His son, Schlo's son, was downstairs, down in the basement, forbidden to attend tonight. Mort, a boy still in Cub Scouts, weeping his heart out.

With the bow tie Mitzi fussed. Getting the two loops balanced. Getting it tight so as to stand up, but not so loose it flopped forward. She said, "Did I ever tell you about the time I was a hero?"

It was a story she'd never told but felt safe telling him. Particularly tonight, before he walked the plank. He and all of Hollywood were walking up that red carpet, smiling and waving while knowing they might be marching into a mass grave. Mitzi could risk telling Schlo. "I tried to help a little girl." With her fingertips she smoothed the lapels of his tux. "I met her in a building, downtown, where she was lost." Mitzi plucked the flower from the velvet tray and pinned it in his buttonhole. A gardenia it was, simple and white and sweet smelling. "I was twelve, and the girl, this lost girl was seven years old. I didn't know what else to do."

Amid all the machinations of her styling, she felt like a mortician. How a mortician must feel primping a dead body.

Schlo slipped a wallet from his back pocket. He took out a couple credit cards and all the cash and left them on the dresser. The wallet he tucked back in his pants, empty except for his driver's license.

She dug into her bag for a small handful of pills and held them cupped in her hand. Schlo pinched up two and downed them with a dash of martini. He pinched up two more and choked them down with the last of his drink. "Now, tell me." He was loose, magnanimous, a generously stoned man beaming over her as if she were his daughter. "How were you the hero of this little lost girl?"

The worst she couldn't tell him, not while the hired car waited to take him to the theater. Why burden what might be his last hours?

Instead Mitzi lifted a comb from the bureau and straightened the part in his hair. She ran the comb over the sides and back of his head. She said, "I took the little girl to meet my father." A speck of dandruff she flicked off his ear. She leaned close and shined each of the studs on his shirt, using her breath and a tissue. "I thought my father could help her."

On television the first of the cars were already arriving at the gateway to the theater. Climbing out and traversing the red carpet were already the first arrivals, looking blue-lipped, looking eyes-dilated from whatever sedatives would get them past their fear. This staggering parade of bejeweled zombies. All of Hollywood royalty, lurching along the red carpet and smiling lazy, crazed, drooling smiles.

And soon Schlo would be staggering into the building alongside them. The most glamorous death march in history.

"Did he?" Schlo asked. "Did your father help this little lost girl you brought home?"

Mitzi watched the television. A young actress in a gown, diaphanous and white as any virgin sacrifice ever wore to be thrown into a volcano, this young woman stumbled and fell to her knees on the carpet. Her face streamed with tears, and she raised jeweled hands to fight off anyone who tried to help her to her feet. As two formally dressed security guards caught her under the arms and began to drag her toward the theater doorway, the camera cut to a smiling newscaster.

On an afterthought Mitzi reached into her bag, again. Instead of pills her fingers plucked out a sealed packet of earplugs. If anything happened, maybe if Schlo couldn't hear he'd have a chance. Like Odysseus plugging the ears of his crew with wax. Maybe if Schlo didn't hear the Sirens he might escape. She offered the packet like she wanted he should take it.

After a look at the earplugs, then at her, he took them and shoved them into his pocket. Looped and sleepy-eyed, Schlo persisted, asking, "Just how did your father help this little lost girl you brought home?"

The panic room amounted to a panic *suite*, five rooms with two full bathrooms. One with a bidet. But after a few weeks of hiding, even with forays into the rest of the house, cabin fever loomed. Just as Blush had said, even a big house still made a very small world.

Tonight they were knee to knee watching television. On the screen a young woman in a shimmering white gown stumbled. She sank to her knees on the red-carpet runway.

"I know her," Blush said, pointing a finger. "She's what's-her-name. The girl who starred in that Civil War picture and got stabbed."

As they watched, two black-suited handlers complete with mirrored aviator sunglasses hoisted the actress by the elbows and dragged her in the direction of the grand theater. First one, then the other silver stiletto slipped from her feet and remained, left behind on the runway as the limp young woman sagged between the two men helping her.

Blush smirked. "Looks as if someone had some pre-party cocktails too many."

Among the Hollywood royalty none looked too happy. Most staggered and lurched with drugged, half-lidded eyes. A few wept, clutching rosaries or prayer beads between prayerful hands. Some Oscar hopefuls carried Bibles. Bibles! Foster marveled. As if they were condemned prisoners walking to the guillotine. This was a level of Academy Award jitters Blush had never seen.

On the television a famous action hero froze at the doorway to the grand theater. As two burly uniformed ushers stepped up to guide him forward, this two-fisted he-man grabbed the doorframe. In what had to be a slapstick comic setup, a third usher hurried in and swung a small truncheon against the actor's handsome head. Knocking him unconscious it would appear. Reducing him to a crumpled pile of evening clothes. It was a brand of offbeat physical humor Foster had never seen at the gala event, and he wondered if the Academy was experimenting with stunts in order to boost their television ratings.

After an interval Blush shouted, "There's Schlo!"

Foster looked.

"You know," she said, "the man who made the baby-sitter bloodbath movie."

Foster looked closer. Here was the man with the voice like so many belches.

Blush leaned close to touch the television. There her producer friend was swaying, none too steadily as he brought up the end of the procession. She said, "He hired the Foley artist who did my scream." Schlo turned slowly to face the dominant camera. As if looking directly at Blush, he seemed to blow her a kiss before toppling through the doorway and out of sight.

PART THREE:
THE PERFECT SCREAM

The buzzer went off. The one for the front door, the street door. A sound Mitzi had almost forgotten, it had been so long since she'd heard it.

Days, she'd kept busy reviewing the inventory of tapes. In the hope that she'd find the master of the scream. The weak, garbled version that people could hear from the Oscar night telecast, it was a squeak, instantly swamped by the combined howling of thousands and the electronic shriek of microphone feedback. To judge from the effect, the recording had been a good one, but it was toast now.

The synchronized limbic systems of three and a half thousand people. All of them spurred to hit the same note, like dogs howling along with a fire engine. Hitting the perfect frequency and volume needed to shatter a building as if it were a champagne glass.

The same way twenty thousand music fans will ride the same limbic wave at a rock concert. To share the same moment of euphoric brain chemistry. Or some fifty thousand fans will pack into a football stadium to share the massive limbic rush created by a winning touchdown. That high isn't available to them sitting alone at home in front of the television.

The Jimmy scream had weaponized people's emotional reaction. It had harnessed their terror. Poor Schlo.

A light blinked on her phone to show one new voicemail. From Schlo's number, a message from that night. A final good-bye. Like those messages left by people before they'd leapt from the World Trade towers. The phone gave the voicemail's length as fifty-three seconds. These last fifty-three seconds of Schlo's life, she couldn't listen to them, not yet.

She'd been letting that light blink for days.

In the sound pit, Mitzi watched the proceedings on live television with the volume muted.

Blush Gentry had staggered out of nowhere clothed only in a shimmering white silk slip. She'd hijacked media attention and the emotions of ten million real-time viewers. A world starving for one ray of sunshine, it glommed onto her. An ambulance nudged its way through the dense crowd. On camera she waved feebly, cradled in the arms of religious leaders who'd abandoned their eulogies to offer themselves as part of a better story. Such a pietà, this near-naked woman lifted on high by collared priests and bearded rabbis and turbaned imams.

As Mitzi's eyes watched Blush ferried away in the ambulance, her ears listened. Through headphones she reviewed one scream after another. Needing to hear only a snippet to know it wasn't Jimmy's.

After a fraction of one scream she switched tracks to hear a fragment of another. Not a scream, but a noise beyond the earphones she almost heard. Hit Pause. Lifted one side of the headset.

She listened to the acoustically dead room. Pea gravel packed in the spaces in the walls to deaden any echoes. The only noise was the electrical ringing in her own head, the room tone of what it meant to be a living human being.

On television the crowds were massed around the police barricades.

Mitzi settled both earphones in place only to hear another noise. Behind the screams, not part of any recording, Mitzi caught the sound of something.

She stopped listening and removed her headphones to hear this new noise.

Mitzi checked the camera for the front door. There stood a dad-shaped stranger, a salesman minus any sample case. Not dressed stiffly like a street preacher. She pressed the intercom, "Yes?"

He looked around until his eyes found the camera mounted on the wall above him. "Hello. Is this Ives Foley Arts?"

The man on camera wore Buddy Holly glasses with lenses so thick they stretched his eyes until each filled the frame. His hair was combed in a good-boy cut, parted on one side and shaved up from the ears. Decent shoes. A handsome catalog face. Something familiar about it, as if she'd seen him on the news. Throwing his voice toward the camera, he said, "I need a scream. People say you're the best."

Haunting her was the idea that we each summon our own death. Some in moments of greatest suffering. Some summon death in their moments of greatest joy and love, out of the awareness that such a moment is a pinnacle never again to be reached.

Perhaps, after all the years she'd gone trolling dive bars and flirting with bottom-feeders in pool halls, her death had come to her door. Wearing glasses.

Mitzi crossed the sound pit, exited to the hallway, went up the flight of stairs to the street level. As she opened the door, she flinched. Unless he had a twin brother, this man she knew.

Through his glasses he regarded her with stunned eyes. His face froze mid-gasp.

It was him from the news. The maniac who'd kidnapped Blush Gentry.

Blush knew the face on Foster's phone but couldn't pin a name to it. So as not to be totally useless, she wrote him a list of local Foley studios. These legacy outfits had been around forever. She'd shown him how to access the panic room so he could sneak back if need be.

In a flash she promised to make good with the bank, and they could be living in the house legit.

To return the favor, he peeled shreds of old duct tape off the seats of his fifteen-hundred-dollar Dodge Dart. These he artfully wrapped around her wrists and ankles, shredding the ends to look frayed and gnawed at.

Like a commuting couple they'd driven into Hollywood, to within a few blocks of the mammoth funeral taking place around the pit that had been the Dolby Theatre. Barefoot and wearing her second-best Victoria's Secret slip, Blush had kissed him good-bye. After all these weeks holed up, she'd cut his hair a few times. Just as he'd washed hers and touched up the roots. And since anything hair-wise was foreplay, they'd had panic room sex. Pass-the-time sex. Nothing-on-television sex.

Stockholm syndrome sex. Although who was keeping whom hostage could be debated.

They'd kissed good-bye in the car, and Blush had hobbled off toward the grieving throngs. About to become a sensation.

For his part, Foster had put on his best tie and the last fresh shirt from his suitcase. A suitcase he'd packed months ago for a trip he'd never taken to Denver. A trip maybe Lucinda herself had foiled. With the list in hand, he'd dropped by a few of the Foley studios. The door for Ives Foley Arts stood in a narrow back street, almost an alley, alone among the back entrances to an Asian restaurant and a tire warehouse. Any parking was between dumpsters.

Bolted to a concrete wall, the sign—"Ives Foley Arts"— its paint had blistered and a tagger had overlapped half of it with spray paint.

It took some looking, but Foster found a push button on the doorframe. He mashed it and heard nothing from within. Not surprising. The building looked to be solid concrete, poured in layers with the wood grain from the forms still visible so long after it had been built.

He mashed the button. Nothing stirred behind the door.

The dumpsters reeked. Foster's was the only car on the street, and he worried how safe it might be. He mashed the button with his thumb.

This time a voice came back, "Yes." A female voice. The sound came from above, so he looked up to find a camera mounted well above the door. He ran a hand down his tie to straighten it and called up to the camera, "I need a scream. People say you're the best."

Her voice sounded scratchy and mechanical through the small speaker.

Nothing followed for a time. No footsteps. No calling out. At last the rattle and clank of metal suggested deadbolts being turned. Stout burglar bars being moved aside. The rattle of door chains being unhooked. The door swung inward.

Framed in the doorway was a woman in her late twenties, possibly thirty years old. Blonde hair, but a shade darker than he'd expected. If she wasn't Lucinda's kidnapper after all these years, she was the kidnapper's sister.

It might've been his imagination, but she seemed to flinch. Her eyes went wide and her teeth showed, clenched.

After that awkward pause, she offered her hand. "Hello," she said.

None of the dark web images had prepared him for this. A small, pregnant woman. Very pregnant. She wore a pair of headphones loose around her neck, a long cable trailing away.

The rage he'd held for so long, it seemed to swell in his hands. The plans he'd made to burn this person alive, to flay the skin of whoever had stolen his child, this fury swelled in his fingers for a moment. Foster might've choked her to death at this door. Swung his fist and crushed her skull. She seemed hardly larger than the girl she'd been in the security video leading Lucinda away.

Instead his hand met hers and they clasped and let go. He managed, "My name's...I'm Gates Foster."

"Hello," the woman in the doorway said, "I'm Mitzi Ives."

Mitzi waved him inside. Motioning down the concrete stairs into the sound pit. His head turned slowly as he took in the equipment, the webs and network of cables and cords that spliced together the jerry-rigged audio components. A cave it was, with the stalactites in the form of mics dropping in dense clusters from the dim ceiling. As stalagmites, floor mics of various heights stood in groups.

The table filled the center of the pit. The mixing board wrapped most of two walls, tier upon tier of dials and switches and meters whose twitching needles registered their every step and breath.

Shadowing him, she chided, "Maybe you don't bullshit me anymore, okay."

She watched as he did his snooping. "Like I told your people, I sell the license for a scream. I never sell my original master."

This Foster circled the room, his head canted back, marveling over the banks of equipment, the ancient analog of everything, sniffing at the burning scent of overheated vacuum tubes and the lingering memory of bleach. He said, "Sorry, lady, I don't have a clue what you're on about."

Mitzi prompted. "It's the magnificent product of your long chain of glorious men." She really stepped on the word *men*.

This man, this Foster, he shrugged. He'd killed Schlo. He'd killed everyone at the Dolby Theatre. For whatever his reason, he'd killed the business.

Mitzi went to the mixing console and grabbed up a ream of pages she'd printed off the web. "Resonance disaster," she said. "That's your game." She'd read the 1850 account of the Angers Bridge, of soldiers marching in step, creating a vibration so strong it buckled the bridge and killed more than two hundred. She shook the pages at him. She ranted about the skywalks in the Kansas City Hyatt, so crowded with dancers in 1981, so many dancers doing the Lindy Hop in synchronized time that the sky bridges had crumbled, killing one hundred fourteen.

A chair she pulled out and swung around for him to take a seat. She pinched an Ambien from the cloisonné plate on the console and slipped it into her mouth. Her tongue felt the smooth, soft promise of it before her molars bit down and ground it to mud. She lifted a wine bottle, then a second, then a third before she found one that wasn't empty. Picking at the cork's wire cage and the foil, she asked, "Champagne?"

This Foster looked away.

She said, "Don't think I don't know why you're here, Mister Deep Operative." She popped the cork. "You're here to tie up loose ends, I'd say. And I'm a loose end, I'm thinking, no?" The printed pages were stacked next to her elbow on the console. She gave them a shove, and the papers spilled and skittered across the floor.

She retrieved three champagne glasses from a shelf and blew the dust from each. Like a witch she felt, pouring champagne into dirty glasses. Waddling around her chilly basement. She offered him a glass of champagne. He took it but didn't drink.

She drank from her own glass to prove it was safe. Champagne and sleeping pills, her baby was being raised on them.

This Foster drank from his. The glass left a line of dirt across his lips. He offered only a search-me shrug. "I'm

looking in particular for a scream used in the movie *Babysitter Bloodbath*."

The buzzer sounded once again. It drew Mitzi's attention to a new image on the monitor. A view of the sidewalk
just outside the building's front door. There stood a young
woman with wavy, dark hair worn across her shoulders.
Around her neck she wore a gleaming double strand of
natural pearls. This figure at the door lifted a finger to
press a button on the doorframe.

"If you'll forgive me," Mitzi said, "I'm expecting
someone for a recording session." She leaned toward a
microphone and said, "Won't you come in, please?" She
touched a button. A door opened at the top of the stairs.
Footsteps descended.

Both the actress and the stranger, this Gates something, they froze at the sight of each other. After the
hesitation the actress, she stepped forward. She extended a
hand, saying pointedly, "My name is Meredith. Meredith
Marshall. And I'm here for an audition."

He accepted her hand. Then jerked his hand away as if
her grip had crushed his fingers.

Mitzi went to the console and brought back the third
glass of champagne. Presenting it, she said, "Perhaps you'd
like a drink before you read for the part?"

To avoid making introductions, Mitzi said flatly, "Mr.
Forester…"

"Foster," he corrected her.

She repeated, "Mr. Foster was just leaving."

* * *

Foster had left. What choice did he have? If he flat out warned this Lucinda that the Foley artist was a kidnapper or worse, he'd never find his kid. And she'd never have believed him. Not after he'd threatened her with a gun. He'd humiliated her.

So he'd left the Foley studio. He'd driven back to the foreclosed house on the ridge. Pulled aside the plywood that hid the street door. Crossed through the vast, dusty chambers. Used the landline in the panic room to call a number he knew by heart.

A voice answered, "Talents Unlimited."

Foster said, "Hello. This is member number 4471."

The voice, a man's voice, asked for a password.

"Pot roast," said Foster.

The voice softened, genial. "What can I do for you, Mr. Foster, my man?"

"You know that girl," Foster began. He stepped up and switched on the room's television. Muted the sound. "I always book the same girl."

Over the phone the sound of keystrokes filled the pause. On television Blush Gentry sat upright in a hospital bed crowded by bouquets of flowers. Billows of orchids and roses. A scene so like Lucinda's funeral.

Over the phone the man said, "Sorry, man, your girl's booked."

Foster watched Blush preen and bat her eyes on the TV. A clear tube fed a needle in her arm. Whatever the painkillers were, they only made her face more smooth and relaxed. Her head lolled, exposing her lovely neck and the cleavage at the top of her lace bed jacket. He told the phone, "That's why I'm calling." He said, "I saw her with some unsavory people. She might be in trouble."

A scroll along the bottom of the television screen announced that the crowdfunding for Blush's medical expenses had topped three million dollars.

The man on the phone laughed. "On the contrary, your girl's on a legit audition."

Blush received an armful of lilies in her hospital bed. Her face and gestures looked so serene, so graceful, the pain meds had to be potent. Her fingertips kept softly touching her cheeks and lips as if feeling for proof she was still alive. The press leaned very near her as if she were answering their questions in a whisper.

Juggling the landline, Foster texted the girl, the latest Lucinda. Or Meredith. Neither one responded.

"You hear me?" the man over the phone said. "This is our girl's break." He explained that a casting director had been calling around. A casting director had been phoning and emailing, trying to book a girl the same age and looks as some missing girl on a milk carton.

The girl on the bed stirred. She blinked slowly, and her lips curved into a loopy, dopey smile. Her bare arms and legs twisted, stretching against the rope that held her wrists and ankles tied to the posts of a bed.

Mitzi lowered a Shure Vocal SM57 until it almost touched the girl's lips. Next to it, an old-school ribbon mic waited. Reaching in from other directions were can mics. A shotgun mic dangled down. Each connected to its own preamp. She waited for the girl to speak, watching for the needles to jump on each of the VU meters.

The needles twitched as the girl spoke. "Are we rolling?" She gave Mitzi a slow-motion, underwater wink. Lifting her chin, she looked down at her exposed breasts, her complete nakedness.

Mitzi nudged a mic closer. "You fell asleep during our talk." In response to a monitor, Mitzi withdrew a mic a smidgen. She said, "I need to check my levels. Meredith, can you tell me what you had for breakfast?"

Still woozy from the sedative, the girl lifted her face toward the Shure. Coming so close she looked at it cross-eyed, she began, "Almonds...yogurt..."

Mitzi chewed another Ambien and washed down the taste with champagne. She considered if she should re-adjust for room tone.

Mitzi pressed on. "Do you know what the Wilhelm scream is, dear?" The girl's eyes found her own.

The girl shook her head.

Mitzi gave the standard lecture. How ordinary people give everything and never see the huge profits generated from their life and death. How even the most intimate moments of our lives are now reproduced and sold as a commodity.

The girl giggled. "Not always," she said. She pulled against the cords binding her, not so much fighting them as pulling against them to stretch her muscles. The meters jumped as she said, "Wylie Gustafson."

In a slurred whisper she described a struggling country singer who'd come to Los Angeles in the 1990s to find success. In a world of hip-hop and rap, his yodeling style of roots music didn't catch on. Among a few odd advertising jobs, he recorded a yodel for a tech start-up, a three-note yodel. They paid him some six hundred bucks for one-time use of it. Two years later, he heard himself yodeling during the Super Bowl, hired a copyright lawyer, and filed a lawsuit for five million dollars. Today he runs a vast horse ranch, paid for by the settlement.

The girl smiled dreamily. "He named his horse Yahoo."

Mitzi couldn't help but smile. For once, it was nice to hear a Hollywood story with a happy ending. An instance when the little man had won.

She stretched a latex glove over one hand. Watching the meters pulse softly, she stretched on the second glove and began to bundle her hair under a cloth surgical cap. She poured another glass of wine and took a few sips with a pill.

The drug's typical side effect had started, the mania. Mitzi reached up and pulled the shotgun mic a skosh closer to the girl's mouth. She asked, "Now tell me what else you ate for breakfast, please."

Her voice reduced to a breath, the girl said, "Black coffee..."

Mitzi tore open a small plastic package containing two foam rubber plugs. With latex fingers she twisted one until it would fit inside of her ear. The small stranger inside her belly shifted and kicked.

Mitzi was unrolling the express envelope, about to remove and unwrap the knife. She had to do this. She had to know if she could commit this horrid act.

The monitors, their needles bounced softly with every sound.

Mitzi patted the girl's shoulder to roust her. She held the girl's gaze and told her, "The name of your character is *Lucinda*..."

The girl's eyes went wide. Pale and suddenly awake, she struggled for real, twisting against her restraints.

Shushing her, telling her to relax, Mitzi said, "Your line...the line I want you to say is 'Help me! Daddy, please, no! Help me!'"

Her breathing shallow and fast, the girl asked, "What's my cue?"

At this Mitzi held the huge knife where the girl's eyes could find it.

So this Foley person had put Foster to work. He'd wanted to buy a scream from the back inventory, so she sat him down at a console and fitted him with a pair of earphones. She lugged an armload of tapes and set them within reach and showed him how to thread each reel. He was to listen his way through a hundred-plus years of screams.

He didn't ask about the actress Lucinda. He couldn't risk spooking this Mitzi person and losing her trust. Fastened around her neck was a double strand of natural pearls that filled him with rage.

She placed a reel on the spindle and threaded the tape. "There's only one scream I want for you to keep," she told him. She drew his attention away from the volume controls and told him, "It's a man screaming from profound agony, I kid you not." She stressed, "At the peak of the scream you'll hear glass breaking. A bottle and a wineglass, breaking."

The rest of the inventory she dismissed with a flick of her wrist, a wave of her hand. The other shrieks were leftovers. Dross.

Then she carted over another stack of reels, and a third. But even with the console piled with reels, each trailing a loose header of tape, this wasn't a divot out of the boxes and file drawers filled with similar recordings.

So Foster had put on his headphones and thrown the switch. The hiss in his ears changed pitch, and a bellowing shriek made him jump to his feet so fast his chair toppled over behind him.

Sitting next to him, her elbow next to his as she listened to her own stack of reels, the Mitzi person shook her head and grinned as if embarrassed on his behalf.

Each scream was over quickly and followed by a

margin of tape hiss. On occasion a man's voice gave instructions. Not always the same man, but clear coaching
directed at the person who was about to scream. The
scream came, shrill and sharp and long. Or ragged and
sobbing.

The tape crackle changed pitch, the signal for a new
scream. Listening for his daughter. Eavesdropping on
these cutting room scraps. The snatches of talk that framed
moments of torture. Torture or terrible acting.

After the tape hiss changed tone yet again, Foster
braced himself for the next assault. Instead, a woman's
voice spoke.

"Of course I'm fucking Schlo," the woman said. Her
voice, the clarity of it, replaced the present moment. Only
this woman from the past existed, shouting, "Untie me
this instant, you'd better!" She shouted, "Do you think
that little baby is your child? Don't make me laugh! That
beautiful little girl is Schlo's!"

He shot a look in Mitzi's direction. To where she was
reviewing and erasing, oblivious to the drama inside his
headset. She might get a kick out of this corny vignette.
More likely she'd heard worse.

The scream dragged on, cursing, ranting, "Walter, you
bastard!" The preserved echo of plain old melodrama.
Leaden dialogue from a trashy movie lost to time. Foster
had to laugh even as the woman's scream faded to silence.
He rewound the section. He hit the Erase button.

* * *

To Mitzi's great relief the wires reached. They unspooled all the way from the console in the sound pit, through storerooms, to the locker. There she'd found the dress.

Not even Ambien could blot out the old memory. Nothing triggered memory better than the smell of that fabric. Nylon tulle and acetate satin stiff with age. The scent of cigarette smoke and hairspray. The stink of mothballs had both poisoned and preserved these, her last memories of her mother.

The light on her phone still blinked: Schlo's last words, still unheard.

The night of the Oscars, first she'd been brave. After that, she couldn't remember.

First she'd donned the dress to crash the awards ceremony. Who doesn't want to play the hero?

Getting in, bypassing the red-carpet protocol had been simple. The security had been too focused on keeping people corralled inside the auditorium, not out. What's more, no one would stop a woman who didn't exist. Even the guards had looked past her. They'd looked through her as if she'd been invisible. Mitzi would've never zippered herself into this dress if she hadn't needed the disguise. The gown featured skirts within skirts within skirts. So many tiers of dry, white satin. She might've been a ghost as she'd roamed up and down the aisles of the Dolby Theatre shouting for Schlo. Shouting for him to plug his ears and escape with her.

Around her neck, in place of a diamond necklace, she'd

worn her noise-canceling headphones. Her skirts she'd lifted as she stalked past people who refused to make eye contact. People with trembling smiles and the crazed eyes of cattle trapped in a slaughterhouse.

A pariah, she'd shouted, "Schlo! You don't have to die!"

A Cassandra, she'd shouted, "Come with me. Take my hand!"

Onstage a young actress, barefoot, had clutched an Academy Award and wept into a microphone. She'd gasped, saying, "I don't want *this*," and shook the statuette. "*I want to live!*" As the orchestra had struck up a fanfare, she'd shouted louder. The music had drowned out her words, and she'd lifted her Oscar. Lifted and flung the flashing, gilded award. Crashing it into the violin section before a pair of men had grabbed her by the thin, bare shoulders and carted her into the wings.

A booming voice had announced the nominees for Best Sound. A film clip had begun as the lights dimmed. The audience had drawn its collective breath, but this hadn't been the scream.

It was then, in the near-dark, a voice had said, "Mitzi, baby girl, are you nuts?" Schlo it was, hissing from where he sat, a few seats off the aisle.

Mitzi had lunged, stumbling over the knees of famous people. She'd reached to get him around one hairy wrist and haul him to his feet.

A wraith, she'd screamed, "I'm here to rescue you!"

A second film clip had begun to play. Another

not-scream. And the audience had released a vast sigh of relief.

Schlo tried to shake her off, but Mitzi had held firm. She'd intended to drag him to safety.

That's when the world had exploded. Something, some force bigger than Ambien and alcohol had struck her. She hadn't saved anyone. What took place next, she couldn't remember. She'd woken up the next morning, dazed, wearing the white dress in an alley in Hollywood.

Her neck had stung. The voicemail on her phone blinked as a clue.

Now she stood to regard the dress as it hung in the locker. These, these flounces of tulle and satin, such a flash fire they were, just waiting to happen. They'd make the best primer for a bomb. Below these Mitzi stacked reels of silver nitrate film. To the brittle skirts she clamped little alligator clips. The clips she spliced to wires. The wires stretched all the way to her doomsday scenario.

Foster tried the phone number once more. For Lucinda. For Meredith Marshall. Neither woman answered.

The dogs howled an ambulance out of the night. As if just by joining forces, every Pomeranian and Chihuahua in the building, every corgi and dachshund in the Fontaine Condominiums, they howled to manifest a siren. The siren created the flashing strobes of red and blue. The lights brought the ambulance to the building's front door, where it idled at the curb.

Reflected in the building across the street, a bright square of light framed a figure drinking wine. The mirrored Mitzi pinched up an Ambien and placed it on her shadow tongue. She tipped back a shadow glass until it was empty.

How her last session had gone, she had no idea. As always, she'd blinked awake to find the actress gone. No blood. No body. A length of tape had spooled from one reel to the other, but she'd not had the heart to listen to herself butchering anyone. She touched the pearls that hid the last faded bruises on her neck. Where the necklace had come from, she had no idea.

She watched out the window as her reflected self fitted earphones on her head. She was listening for clues about her mother. About the death of her father. Any extra chatter on the tapes that might fill the gaps in her memory. To answer the questions she had about how she'd arrived at this place in her life. On the street, the paramedics were unloading a gurney and bumping it up the front steps.

The reflected her poured a new glass of wine. A shadow finger reached to press Play on her media player. A voice filled her head. The voice of a child, it blotted out any reality of the present.

Bright, bright and clear, clear and soft, the voice said, "My name? My name is Lucinda Foster."

A man's voice followed. The voice of Mitzi's father, as

blocky as his handwriting, said, "Would you like to be in a movie, Lucinda?" The question rose and fell in volume as if he were turning away and not giving her his full attention.

"My name is Lucy," said the girl. "My mother's name is Amber. Amber and Gates Foster are my mom and dad."

Mitzi stopped the tape. Rewound a section. Hit Play.

"...and Gates Foster are my..."

She repeated the process to be certain.

"...Gates Foster are..."

The girl on the milk carton. The girl Mitzi had been trying to remember for so long. Someone else had been looking for her, the man she'd been working beside for the past few days. This man who'd come to her studio slinking like an ears-back dog, asking if he could buy an old scream. Gates Foster. Not the Oscar-night scream.

The baby kicked, and her breasts began to leak. To quell the acid reflux she downed another pill with more wine.

She watched her shadow self press Play.

Her father's voice said, "Your father is coming for you right now."

The child asked, "Where's my friend?" She asked, "Where's Mitzi?"

The reflection across the way froze with a wineglass held halfway to her mouth.

Protesting, the child's words began to falter as her voice in Mitzi's head said, "Where did Mitzi go?"

In a soft voice the man shushed her. From experience,

Mitzi knew he'd be watching the monitor in the studio. He'd be toying with the levels. Adjusting the mics.

The girl said, "Tell Mitzi that I don't like this game."

At that, Mitzi rewound the tape. She rewound the tape and erased all of it.

Foster could almost peg the speaker. The voice on the tape, a man's voice. He rewound a section, glanced at Mitzi Ives working at his elbow, deaf to anything beyond her headphones. He adjusted his own headphones. Pressed Play.

"Jeez, doc," the man said, "did you have to dirty every knife in the prop room?" Someone else laughed. Several men.

He rewound. Pressed Play. "…dirty every knife in the prop room?" The laughing.

Foster listened until the tape ran out. Rewound, again. He hit Pause after certain words, after "every," after "room." Two faces would almost come into focus. Two of the few people he considered friends. He ran an inventory of the men at his office. He surfed his memory for a sound bite of Amber's father, Paul, and pulled up a snippet. Paul saying, "Merry Christmas!" big and bold at the front door to their house while his wife, Linda, crouched down to hug Lucy.

The voice wasn't Paul's. It was no one at the office.

Those were the limits of his life. Then the support group occurred to him. When he ran the faces through his mind, both voices fit as perfectly as a key sliding into a lock. He wondered if there might be voice twins, vocal doppelgangers. Any two men in the world who shared the same voice as exactly as they might share the same finger-print. The two men on the tape, it couldn't be. It would be impossible. Foster erased the tape, but the truth of what he had to do next crushed him. It bowed his head and slumped his shoulders. The miserable task that lay before him after the sun set that day.

Mitzi built a garden. When the stranger growing inside her fussed, she did just as her father had done and set up a cot in the sound pit. Within reach of the mixing board, she heaped the cot with old blankets and lay back upon their musty softness, the smell of basement drains and damp laundry left too long in the washer. She stretched an arm to shut off the studio lights, bank by bank, until the dark and silence were absolute. Doing so, she erased the world so she could build it anew.

The stranger within her held still as if curious. Waiting.

As her father had done, Mitzi found knobs by touch alone. She lowered the room temperature. She cued a chorus of nighttime crickets. She brought up the sound of peeping tree frogs. The gushing sound of water she adjusted to a trickle. A melodious trickle like a fountain. The fountain's tinkle she matched with the sound of wind chimes.

Out of the black, silent void she built the world of a nighttime paradise. Mice rustled through fallen leaves. Tree branches creaked and scraped in the breeze, and an owl hooted twice and took wing through the air above them.

Just as her father had done, Mitzi introduced a quiet family of deer that nipped at rose bushes and snapped off the tender buds. She replaced the flawed, troubled world with tall grass that whispered its blades together.

In this, this soundproof, lightless void, she conjured a paradise. And soon the stranger within her seemed to fall asleep. And as the tinkle of water and wind chimes ran on their endless loop, Mitzi, on her nest of moldering blankets, even she fell asleep.

Foster moved aside the basketball. Gently, he picked up each Teddy bear and carried it a safe distance. As he lifted a stuffed giraffe, it began to play a music box lullaby, a tinkling melody that sounded big in the cold night. The bright notes shrill and unnerving as they echoed back from the surrounding tombstones. To silence the giraffe, he lay it across the grave and beat it with the curved blade of his shovel.

He gathered and set aside the holiday cards, the birthday cards and glass-encased candles labeled with pictures of saints. Pictures of Christ cradling a lamb in his arms. Their wicks burnt down to black stubs, the candles sloshed with water collected from the lawn sprinklers. The plush toys were furred with grass clippings thrown up by the lawn mowers.

Fully uncovered, the headstone glowed in the moonless

dark. Trevor Laurence, beloved son of Robb and Mai Laurence. The birth and death dates only months apart.

Foster knelt in front of the grave marker and whispered, "If I'm wrong, I'm very sorry." He stood and stomped the blade of the shovel into the soft grass. Using the spade, he cut the sod and set it aside in neat squares. Atop these he spread a tarp to collect the loose dirt. With every few shovelfuls he froze and listened. The crickets and frogs had stopped, but now they sang anew. Their din almost drowned out his heavy breathing as he heaved a spade of dirt out of the growing pit. He dug the soil out from beneath his feet until only his head rose above the lip of the hole. Then the shovel struck concrete, the concrete vault to protect the casket. With his bare hands, his fingers caked in wet earth, Foster brushed the edges of the vault lid clean.

He'd seen pictures. Members of the support group had passed photographs from hand to hand. Robb had shown them a tiny casket of polished rosewood that glowed almost red. Hardly the size of a suitcase. Pictures of Mai and her family tossing flowers into the open grave. No pictures of the body, but there wouldn't be, not after Trevor's daylong suffering in a hot car.

The same way Blush had used the sharp end of the lug wrench to pry away plywood, Foster stabbed it under the vault lid and muscled the concrete. He told himself this was only a movie. He was only a character in a cheap drive-in-theater horror movie. The lid tipped up and slid aside, revealing the casket that seemed smaller than it had looked in the photographs. Movie or not, the casket lid wouldn't open. It needed a key. A socket deal. Otherwise the lid was locked down to make it watertight.

Careful not to step on the casket itself, he planted his feet on the concrete edges of the vault. Movie or not, he reared back with the shovel and swung it down like an axe. The blade sinking into the varnished wood, wood even now so red he half expected it to bleed. A second blow split the casket lid. A third tore the lid down the center, and Foster dropped to his knees and clawed at the splintered wood. Tearing aside the satin and padding. Ready to see, hoping to find the sad horror, the tragic withered body. He ripped away the padded and pleated lining.

Under the weak beam of his flashlight his hands tossed back the quilted satin blanket and pillow. Buried here and honored with toys, wept over in photographs, inside this beautiful shattered casket Foster found nothing. The little mattress was unstained.

Even here, sunk a man's height into the damp soil of a graveyard, his phone got a signal. He dialed.

A voice answered, the voice from the tape he'd erased in the studio said, "Hello?"

"Friend," said Foster.

After a blip, a breath, a shudder, after a beat of nothing, Robb Laurence said, "Gates." He asked, "Where are you calling from?"

Foster asked, "Is the support group still meeting on Thursdays?"

Over the phone Robb said, "Are you okay?"

"Are you going to group this week?" asked Foster.

Robb answered too loud. As if getting someone's attention, he said, "Am I going to the support group, you mean?" As if there might be someone there to triangulate the call and locate Foster.

"That's exactly what I mean," Foster said, and broke the connection.

Mitzi opened a third bottle of wine before she could listen to the voicemail.

She'd seen some of the video shot inside the Dolby Theatre that night. Bits had played on television, the cleaner bits. The worst were on the web, but she'd not gone to look there. Alone in her condo, she set her phone on the desk in front of her and pressed Play.

The recording replaced the world around her.

"Mitz," a voice croaked. "My baby girl."

A voice from the grave, it gave her gooseflesh all up her arms.

It continued, "Mitz, it's good you don't pick up." Like a man shouting at the hands-free phone in his car, it said, "God forbid you should pick up and hear this." Screams, human screams and a noise like thunder muffled his words. "...so much dust a person can't breathe," Schlo shouted. "Can you hear it?"

THE INVENTION OF SOUND

Mitzi pictured the footage from inside the Imperial Theater. Cracks running through every surface, cracks branching into more cracks. The walls and ceiling shifting. Crumbling. Thick dust sifting and settling over everything below.

"Choking I am. Mitzi, my baby girl, I want you should know how proud I am for you. A good life I've lived." He paused, cleared his throat. "Words can't go there, but the balconies, they're pancaking together. Oh, the horror of so many...just gone."

The screams diminished, but now the thunder of steel bending and glass breaking grew louder.

Mitzi could picture this from the video she'd seen on the news. The concrete slabs of the walls had fractured into chunks, shattered into pieces, busted into rocks of cement already blasting into sand. "So much dust," Schlo said. He coughed into the phone. "I should suffocate before I get smashed. Blinded I am, half blind from such dust!"

Mitzi shook tears from her eyes.

"Baby girl," Schlo's voice continued, hoarse, "I love that you tried to rescue me. I swear by all the blood of all the martyrs that I didn't know." He asked, "How was I to know?"

Schlo, like all the people she'd loved, now reduced to a recording.

It was too much.

In the last moment of his life, Mitzi lost her nerve.

To keep from hearing her friend die she switched off the phone.

The voice belched and gasped. His breathing bubbled and gargled. In nasal tones the man on the tape panted, fast, panted-panted as if his lungs had shrunken to dime sized. Over Foster's headphones he gurgled and coughed as if his chest were filling with water.

He moaned, "My sweet girl." He spat, and a stream of something liquid splashed against something flat and hard. Clearer now, he said, "Everything I've done I've done..." He swallowed. "To coax you to this moment."

Foster tried to plug the man's voice into a movie. Some drama about a sinus infection sufferer. An Academy Award winner about a severe head cold.

Within the headphones the man took a long, ragged breath. "You're not to blame," he said, his voice hardly rising above a whisper. "I've groomed you to do this since the day you were born." He said, "I know the terrible power you feel at this moment."

In the darkness of Foster's mind, the man gagged. He vomited an invisible stream, of what Foster couldn't imagine. Gobbets and clots spattered in some long-ago sickroom. Every sound rang with a bright echo that suggested concrete or tile. Nothing soft. In the background he could hear a child, a young person, sobbing.

His airway cleared, the man spoke louder. He said, "One day, when you're my age an apprentice will appear."

Foster risked a sideways look at Mitzi Ives. He wanted to wave, to ask her if she knew these characters. What melodramatic soap opera was this from?

Oblivious in her headphones, Mitzi was mouthing silent words. As if saying her prayers or learning a foreign language. She sat with her knees tucked under the mixing console, as close as her belly allowed. With one hand she petted herself, running her fingers in long strokes over the swelling shape of her unborn child.

The man in Foster's head panted for air, panting out the words "Do not be afraid." He said, "Your apprentice, one day he will do this exact same thing to you."

Foster touched a knob to sharpen the tone. Turned a dial to up the volume.

His voice fading, the man said, "On the day when you are chained in my place, you must remember how proud I am of you." He gasped, "May you die feeling so much pride." Here the voice rasped and went quiet.

Replacing the man's words was only room tone and a steady drip-drip-drip that slowed to one final drop.

At that, Gates Foster rewound the tape and hit Erase.

The tape ended, but Mitzi pretended to still hear something. Her pulse she could hear. She pretended she could hear a second heartbeat, the baby's.

The Foster person sat cocooned in his headphones. He might cast a glance in her direction, but he couldn't hear as she whispered to her child. To the child she would never meet. She whispered, "Do not be afraid. You will be raised by a woman who loves you, but that woman will not be me."

She stroked and petted the shifting mound at her waist, telling it, "You will be part of a family, but not my family. My family will die with me. Our work must die with me."

Mitzi touched the tiny hand that pressed to touch hers. Without bitterness, she told the child, "You will step into a destiny that will not be the destiny I was tricked into fulfilling."

Before the next length of tape would deliver the next scream, the next gasping, choking bellow of fear and pain, Mitzi continued to whisper to the infant that held still and even now seemed to listen and understand.

As Foster listened, this Foley person explained how people find the source of a sound. With low-frequency sounds, the human brain analyzes the time delay between when the sound reaches each of the two ears. But with high-frequency sounds the brain analyzes the loss in volume between when the sound reaches each ear.

In this way Mitzi Ives was training him. Her voice, calm, a master schooling her apprentice. Tutoring him. She passed along what seemed a lifetime of knowledge, several lifetimes. A legacy.

"You never hear a dry voice, not anymore," she said. By that she meant that every song and soundtrack has been sweetened or made more warm and rich. Or the voice has been tweaked to sound more tubby, the reverberation has been lengthened or shortened. She talked about the decay time of a sound. She taught him how to manipulate the fatness of a sound.

According to her father, to stories he'd told her, any wire fence could hold a recording. She described how a person could walk along a fence and use a microphone attached to a needle that would encode her voice along the wire. As a child, she said, she'd spliced a set of headphones to a needle and walked along random wire fences trying to read any secret messages. Barbed wire fences. Chain link.

Likewise, she explained how any speaker could be reverse wired to work as a microphone. This created such a wonderful distortion that musicians recorded their work through speakers intentionally.

She described how crooning had replaced more traditional singing in the 1920s. At the time, carbon would build up in microphones and broadcasters needed to shut off each mic, occasionally, and strike it with a small hammer to clear that buildup. The softer, more prolonged notes sung by crooners created less carbon buildup. Cornets replaced trumpets for the same reason. In short, people could only listen to what microphones could pick up. Technology dictated fashions in music.

Mitzi Ives introduced him to ribbon mics and moving coil mics, carbon mics and electrostatic mics. She taught him about parabolic, omnidirectional, and bidirectional mics. The racks of analog mixing equipment. She showed him vacuum tubes that would cost five thousand dollars to replace, and microphones worth twenty thousand. She toured him through concrete bunkers lined with file cabinets filled with recordings.

She told him about the Wilhelm scream.

Through this warren of rooms ran a pair of wires, just two wires routed along the floor. Their tour followed these wires, but she never called his attention to them. In the farthest reaches of the basement the wires disappeared into a closed locker. Foster opened the door. Inside hung something shapeless and white. Shoved into the locker and hung on a hook, it was a dress. Satin and ruffles as fancy as a wedding cake.

Like a fuse, the wires looped up to clips attached to the skirts. Two metal clips clamped to the fabric and to each other. Beneath the dress, a stack of rusted film reels stank of vinegar.

Mitzi Ives waited, but he didn't ask. He closed the locker, and she continued his education.

It didn't sound like much on the web. The cell phone videos from inside the Dolby Theatre on Oscar night, they sounded thin. Screechy. Nothing like Mitzi knew the Jimmy scream would sound on the master tape. These were crude copies. In one clip banked rows of glittering celebrities sat, their heads thrown back, their mouths gaping in a mutual choir of shrieks. Dogs howling. A few among them stood, their necks corded with effort, teeth bared, screaming as debris bombarded them, culminating in the concrete wall behind them crashing over everything like a tidal wave.

Mitzi clicked to another clip. Another choir of wailing faces. She paused the video and expanded it to fill the screen. She studied the faces, each distorted. Each chin dropped to each chest, each mouth stretched so taut the lips looked thin and white. Nobody dodged or ducked as shattered lighting and bricks hammered down upon them. How many clips she'd watched she had no idea. She would watch every post before she'd ever give up hope.

In one clip a white-dressed figure dashed through the shot, screaming, "Schlo, you don't have to die!" No one in the surrounding seats gave the figure a glance. A woman, her white dress billowed around her, the wide skirts filled the aisle. She shouted, "Schlo, take my hand!"

In a different clip the deranged woman forced her way past seated guests and yanked at the wrist of a man. Unseen by her, two uniformed security guards came down the aisle from behind. One leveled something, not a gun, but something like a gun, and pulled the trigger. A wire jetted through the air and lanced the back of the lunatic's neck.

In a third clip the woman shrieked. Clearly tasered, she thrashed and screamed as the guards carried her twitching body away. The video clip followed along until they disappeared through a fire exit. That, that's how Mitzi had found herself dressed in ragged white satin, sitting in a Hollywood alley the morning after the disaster.

Watching now, her neck ached. The Taser explained the mark she'd found. Here was everything that she couldn't remember.

She hunched with her nose almost touching the screen. Besides the network cameras, cell phones had recorded the final moments from every angle. Never had so many people documented their own demise.

To know the pecking order helped. In effect, to know where the VIPs among the VIPs were seated. Scanning through the center of the main floor, Mitzi paused. She backtracked a moment, and there he sat. The gardenia fresh in his lapel. His hand held his phone to his face as he spoke, as he left the voicemail. There were the malachite cuff links. There was the Timex watch. Here the walls and ceiling weren't crashing down. Instead, the floor buckled. A sinkhole opened, swallowing seated movie stars near Schlo. The fissure yawned and more A-listers tumbled in, screaming. They poured down into whatever basements or parking garages lay below the auditorium. Schlo continued to talk on his phone. Even as his own seat tipped sideways and tumbled toward the void, he was still talking, trying to leave something of himself for her benefit in the physical world.

Here she touched her phone to start the voicemail. Schlo's voice shouted, "Glad I am that you're safe, that my family is safe." He was shouting because of the roar around him or because he'd plugged his ears. Or shouting maybe just because Schlo always shouted on the phone, but he told her, "Now's the time we should talk turkey, Mitz. And by that I'm telling you—destroy your damn tape!"

The end looked fast. Fast and painless. Painless and complete.

The tiny figure on the video shouted into his phone, "If our deaths are to mean anything, you should destroy what you've brought into this world!"

That was Schlo. That was Schlo all over, still yelling into his phone even while his entire world tilted sideways and he was tossed into oblivion.

Foster tried the knob, but it wouldn't turn. Through the basement windows he could see inside. Dust coated the floor of the room where they usually met, a thin layer of dust unmarked by footprints. Gone was the usual circle of folding chairs. Gone was the sign in the window that welcomed the parents of missing or deceased children. To stand at the bottom of the concrete steps leading down from the sidewalk, this felt too much like standing in a grave, so Foster walked up to street level. There his beater Dodge sat at the curb, the only car on the block. Traffic passed a couple streets away on the avenue. Footsteps grew from that direction.

A figure moved along the brick walls, becoming a man, becoming Robb. Robb calling, "It's too late, you know." At such a distance he had to yell, "You can't stop anything."

Foster guessed his name wasn't actually Robb. Nobody he'd met at this support group had been anybody. This place wasn't a place, and it never had been. He took his best shot. "It was just me, wasn't it?" He called out, "Why me?"

Robb, no longer the leader of a group that had never existed, he stopped out of reach. "You showed up is all." Patronizing, his smile smug and guilty at the same time, he said, "We set a trap, and one day you stepped into it."

They'd all been actors or mercenaries. There to stage the kind of a scam called a Big Store. A long con. They'd each faked a dead child, rehearsing their stories together. On the first evening when Foster had come down the stairs from the sidewalk and read the sign and opened that door, they'd all looked up as someone among them had been recounting a death that had never taken place. Someone had waved him inside. Whoever had been telling their story began to fake weeping, and Foster had been completely suckered. He asked, "There had to be other grieving parents, so why me?"

Robb, not-Robb, the voice on the tape complaining about too much blood and too many knives to clean, he shrugged. "You're a man. We needed someone of your size."

Foster felt the gun in his jacket pocket.

"And we needed someone who was angry," said not-Robb. "We could channel your anger."

The funeral is what he referred to. The mob scene, it had all been arranged to drive Foster into action. Something besides Lucinda had been steering his course, these people, but for their own purpose.

"Don't take any of this personally," not-Robb said. His smugness fell away. He ducked his head and scratched at the back of his scalp. "Our assignment was to rope in someone ruthless, with a bottomless rage that would feed his work for years to come." He looked around, his eyes fixing on something. "The best agent is an agent who doesn't know he's one."

When Foster looked, the something was just a window. Only curtains moving in a window.

Not-Robb stepped against the side of the building as if trying to blend into the brick wall. "I'm only here to deliver a message." He shot another look at the curtains. "Tell your boss…"

Foster asked, "What boss?"

"Tell Mitzi Ives," not-Robb clarified, "that she has until Tuesday to turn over the asset in question."

A new figure was approaching. Another man, a shaggy-haired stranger, slowing as he drew near. Some hemp-headed caveman throwback.

Not-Robb followed Foster's gaze to this new stranger, a burner type, but lanky. "Tuesday at four o'clock," not-Robb said. "That's when my employer will arrive to seize the asset by force."

Foster asked, "What asset?"

Already backing away, retreating, not-Robb said, "Your boss will know. Tell her to deliver the asset before it's too late." And at that he'd turned his back and was jogging into the distance. Even as the new stranger strode up, not-Robb broke into a sprint and disappeared.

For an instant the new man seemed to be walking past. A love-beaded granola type, he scowled. His shoulders bunched, his hands were balled into fists. The man's arm lashed out, landing a fast, hard crack against the side of Foster's skull. A strobe flashed behind Foster's eyes, and his knees gave way. He caught the sidewalk hard, landing on his ass. With the impact of the man's fist the gun tumbled from Foster's pocket. Tumbled and clattered across the sidewalk. Clattered and skidded over the curb. Skidded and dropped into a storm drain.

The gun, gone. The man, the man kept walking away. Not a stranger, not entirely. Not anymore.

The stink of patchouli and the words "Harsh, dude" sprang briefly to mind.

Mitzi arrived at the diner wearing the pearls. The booth near the back. The usual arrangement. An actress, a friend, sat waiting. Mitzi slipped into the booth and asked, "You called about a job?"

Blush Gentry didn't answer, not right away. From behind oversized sunglasses she stared at Mitzi's swollen belly. "You're lucky," she said. "I wish I could have a kid."

It was clear to Mitzi that Blush had arranged her own

kidnapping as an excuse not to attend the Oscar ceremony. She said, "You could have a child with your kidnapper."

"Not him." Gentry shook her head. "Too old. He's shooting nothing but hot water and birth defects, you know?"

A server approached the table. A young woman, part of the new influx of pretty hopefuls migrating to California to revitalize the movie business. Mitzi regarded this one as eager but hopeless. When the advent of sound had killed off a generation of silent stars, their replacements had been recruited from live theater in New York. The theater would once more provide the new stars.

Blush removed her sunglasses. The server's eyes came to rest on the actress and couldn't look away. Starstruck, she asked, "What can I start you with?"

"Nothing, sweetheart," said Gentry. "Maybe coffee."

Mitzi asked for a glass of wine. White wine. It was lunch. Just wine, a big pour.

The server stared at the pregnant belly, obviously trapped between asking if someone was pregnant or implying Mitzi was fat. She didn't risk it. "We have a Syrah."

"Make that two," Blush said. When the server had left, the actress plucked a napkin from a dispenser on the table and began folding and worrying the paper. Without meeting Mitzi's gaze, she said, "Certain persons have impressed upon me that you're in illegal possession of an asset." Blush's delivery was wooden and halting. "These...persons have asked me to intervene at this juncture." An actress reading a script as if English were not her first language. "If you've not relinquished said asset by Tuesday at four o'clock, said persons will arrive at your place of business to forcibly take custody."

As rough as the delivery sounded, Mitzi understood. Someone was going to raid the studio. Special forces would ransack Ives Foley Arts on Tuesday afternoon.

As the server brought their wine, Mitzi reached both hands to the back of her own neck. She undid the clasp and gathered the double strand of pearls cupped in one palm. "Until you have a baby of your own," she said, and handed the necklace across the table.

Speechless, Blush lifted the two ends and fastened them together around her own neck.

They'd set Foster up, total strangers. They'd bullied him into staging that fake funeral, the carnival freak show, and they'd driven him to explode. Amber had been there, a witness seated in the back. Some crew of people had ambushed him with cell phones in a staged nightmare that had in fact been a plot right up to the email link to the babysitter movie. It sounded crazy, but he was part of something, targeted by something. Strangers had hijacked his anger and grief. Telling it now to Amber, Foster knew that he sounded crazy, too.

Mission accomplished.

Amber kissed his forehead, gently forcing his head down onto a pillow. To find her meant calling her father.

And just by chance she'd picked up the phone, and after a moment's embarrassment Amber had explained that she was hiding out from publicity, hiding from the media at her father's house, at Paul's house in the suburbs. And after another moment of embarrassed silence she'd asked him to stop by. And here he was, guided by his ex-wife into a back bedroom and told to sit on the bed and calm down.

"Rest," she whispered into his hair. Her fingers lifted off his glasses, folded them and set them on a windowsill.

Amber's dog jumped up on the bed beside him. A small dog. A pug. Maybe it was Paul's dog, Foster didn't know.

"They stage-managed everything," he tried to explain. Minus his glasses, the room swam out of focus.

Amber listened like she did. She let him run out of steam. Reaching toward the foot of the bed, she spread a blanket to cover him. To bind him down, she tucked the edges in around his arms and shoulders. This done, she went to the room's window and looked outside before drawing the curtains. The pug dog snuggled in tight against his leg.

Peering outside around one edge of the curtains, she said, "You need to rest. Just for an hour."

What a stroke of good fortune. Maybe his luck was turning around. To connect with Amber when he needed her most. And to find her at the first place he called, and to be invited over and given a place to sleep. The dirt from Trevor's grave clung to his pants in dark scabs. It lined his fingernails. But baby Trevor had never existed. Robb was a character, and most of the world had turned into a movie where events were prompted to move him toward some goal. He felt his bones settling into the mattress. Amber leaned down to kiss him again, and her hair fell forward to brush his face.

"Sleep," she said. She padded quietly to the doorway and quit the room, pulling the door closed behind her.

Whatever had trapped him, Foster had escaped. Here he was safe. Tuesday at four o'clock something, some long con would descend on Mitzi Ives, but he didn't have to be there.

He could sleep through Tuesday, he felt that tired. The dog wedged against him felt almost like Lucy had as a baby. To have the smell of Amber, of her hair, clinging to him, he could imagine when they were first married. He placed himself back in a time when they were happy, and the future glowed. The baby snuggled close into his hip, and if he didn't open his eyes he was a new father, a young man.

If he didn't open his eyes, the world seemed perfect.

Soft and low, the little dog began to howl. Then long and loud, the howl heralded a siren. A siren joined the dog's howl, and from beyond the bedroom window a chorus of neighborhood dogs joined the siren. A police car approached, drawing so close it drowned out the animals.

Foster opened his eyes and retrieved his glasses.

The pug watched, head cocked, as Foster pulled open

the curtains and the window and slipped quietly into the backyard. Slipped over the sill and jumped to the grass. Jumped and vaulted the back fence. Vaulted and raced away down an alley.

Mitzi put Foster aboard a ship. The scenario had always been one of her favorites. She shut off the studio lights and began to build the world by creating the ocean. The mid-Atlantic in March, a storm-tossed, wind-churned ocean. She broke waves against the wooden hull and whistled the wind through the rigging. She made the canvas sails billow and snap. Rain strafed the decks, and water sloshed in the bilges.

He'd staggered in, this Gates Foster, exhausted and mumbling. His clothes caked with dirt. A purple goose egg swelling one side of his face. Mumbling about a conspiracy. Mumbling about being betrayed by his former wife.

She'd dragged out the cot and blankets and urged him to lie down. She deleted this world and began to build a new one around him. Lightning cracked. Thunder roared. And gradually the distance between the thunder and lightning lengthened. The winds weakened. Of the heavy rain only a light mist fell on the ship. Then even the mist stopped. The sails fell slack as the seas calmed, and by that point this Gates Foster had fallen fast asleep.

The day dragged on. Each scream might be the pain and terror of someone, but it wasn't the scream Foster was looking for. It wasn't the scream of anyone he loved. And as his reserve of empathy ran dry, he found himself irked by the noise of people's suffering. This bedlam crop of people's misery, he began to hate the strangers whose torture hurt his ears.

Foster reviewed each scream. Dismissed and deleted it. Moved on to the next.

Mitzi had cast looks at him, almost frightened looks. Almost as if she knew who he was and what he intended to do.

He texted the escort agency and got no reply.

He erased the agony of another reel filled with an army of dying strangers.

Yelling to be heard, he pushed back from the console and asked, "When are you due?"

When Mitzi didn't respond, isolated by her own set of headphones, he tried again.

She turned, pulling the headphones down to her neck.

"When's the baby due?" he asked.

Mitzi shrugged. "Tuesday afternoon," she said. "Just after four o'clock." She placed the headphones back over her ears and returned to the task at hand.

In Foster's headset the tape hiss changed. The tone shifted to suggest a new recording. A different room tone brought a man's voice. This stranger said, "Mitzi, honey, you were wrong to tie up Daddy while he was asleep..."

Foster snuck a glance at the woman working next to him.

A child's whisper answered him. It was lost in the tape hiss until Foster could make out the words, "...what did you do to my friend?"

The man stammered, "Mitzi, you can't."

The child's voice shrieked. Raging, "Into the microphone, please!"

His voice reedy and shrill, the man insisted, "You can't. Mitzi, you love me!"

As silence fell, Foster listened harder. He recognized the voices as something, as being related to something he'd heard before. A pickup from a different microphone? Another fragment of the past.

Whatever the case it wasn't his past.

He checked the label on the reel, the list of names for each recording. In the loopy handwriting of a teenager, this one was titled *Serial Killer Flayed to Death by Child.* He rewound the segment. He erased it. He waited for the next.

Mitzi knew the primitives were right. The tribes who believed a photograph would steal a person's soul. It would, and it did. So did an audio recording, as did video. Our greatest creation is our selves. The way we cultivate our appearance and behavior. And nowhere is our artwork more apparent than in our minds. The way we each have an idea of self. The one perfect self we've chosen by rejecting all other options.

The opportunity costs of identity.

We've rejected the slack self, the fat self, the gray-haired or skinny self, those constant other selves we see modeled by people around us.

We are each our own best effort. And we're satisfied until we see a photograph or hear a recording of our voice. All the worse is the torture of video, to witness the squawking, gawky monster we've created. The you that you've chosen from all possible yous to create. The one life you've been given, and you've dedicated it to perfecting this staggering yammering artificial Frankenstein's monster stitched together from the traits of other people. Anything original, anything innately you, it's long ago been discarded.

Knowing all of that, Mitzi still pressed Play.

How the session had gone, Mitzi had no idea. As always she'd blinked awake to find the actress gone. No blood. No body. Only the faint perpetual whiff of bleach. A length of tape had spooled from one reel to the other, but she'd not had the heart to review the result.

Now the reel turned, and a girl's voice said, "He named his horse Yahoo."

Through her headphones Mitzi recognized the snap of a latex glove. She heard wine poured into a glass. Her recorded voice sounded slurred. In slow-motion words, she said, "The name of your character is *Lucinda...*"

The meters registered something. A jump or the creak of the ropes.

Shushing her, telling her to relax, Mitzi said, "Your

line…the line I want you to say is 'Help me! Daddy, please, no! Help me!'"

Almost inaudible on the tape, the girl asked, "What's my cue?"

At the console, Mitzi lowered the volume just as a scream rang out. The shrieks built in stages and broke with a ragged gasp followed by a hoarse coughing fit. After that came the silence of death.

Rising in the background were sobs. Sobbing, a woman crying softly, the bright ding of a knife dropped on the concrete floor. A self Mitzi didn't remember.

Another woman, the girl's voice asked, "Can you untie me, please?"

The sobs ebbed to sniffing, shuddering sighs. Halting exhales.

"I'm going now," the young woman said. "Here," she added, "take these. They're real pearls." A click followed, too faint for anything but the most sensitive mic to catch. Then footsteps hurried away. A door opened, closed.

Listening to the tape now, those echoed voices seemed more real than the man working next to her. More real than the stranger curled up inside of her. Mitzi sat motionless, the headphones cupped over her ears, and listened to her real self weeping before the artificial her reached forward to hit Erase.

From **Oscarpocalypse Now** *by Blush Gentry (p. 205)*

Why did I go with Gates? He rescued me from the real kidnappers. Millions of people don't know what goes into ranch dressing, billions of people, but they still love eating it. I don't recall any detail of my kidnapping, but I know that Gates Foster rescued me and I married him and now he's among the industry's leading Foley artists. They headhunted him, the government did, as part of their effort to rebuild the domestic film industry. And I know I love him—even though half the time he smells like bleach—and I love our son, Lawton. Almost as much as I love chromium diopside. I mean, you just put on any of my high-fashion rings or necklaces and it's like you're in a classic Hollywood movie. You know?

You could say I'm married to chromium diopside. I was born to be married to chromium diopside.

Foster wiped another tape. How many screams he couldn't say. He'd quit counting.

Lucinda had never seemed more lost to him. He'd tracked her this far, to this concrete pit in the basement of a soundproof, world-proof bunker, and now he was forced to search for her among the screams of so many. The hell was inside his head where he met the ghosts and sorted between them. As if he were groping through the underworld seeking just one soul from amongst the billions of dead.

He mounted another reel on the spindle and threaded the tape. The headphones hissed. His fingers lowered the volume by twisting a knob the moment before a scream ripped through his head. A long one, someone with huge lungs, the scream ran for longer than most. It ran for too long. Until it was no longer a scream.

He turned to meet the Mitzi person's round, shocked eyes. She'd lowered her headset, and as he did the same the scream continued. It filled the studio.

"My alarm," she shouted against the noise that burst from speakers in every corner. Tuesday had arrived.

"They've come for their invention." She threw him a smug look and reached across the console to flip a switch. Just that one unmarked, unremarkable switch, just the click of it and the studio began to fill with the smell of smoke. The bitter stink after a million birthday candles are blown out.

Whether the street camera had been blacked out with paint or busted off, the monitor showed nothing. Something slammed against the outside of the street door, that metal door that looked stronger than the concrete walls surrounding it.

Mitzi's plan wasn't a plan. Not really. Not until she stood up and walked to the door of the prop room. There among the machetes and sabers she found a length of steel chain and a padlock. There she found the Carving-ware knife.

The screams of everyone layered and overlapping, they blared. Smoke, acrid, stink-smelling, black and poisonous, it seeped from the boxes and the file drawers. Behind the smoke the first orange suggestions of flame. The pounding at the door almost lost in the din.

Mitzi carried the chain and her glass of wine to the table in the center of the room and lay down across it. The stranger inside of her fought to escape. As she wrapped the chain around her legs, binding her thighs tight together and snapping the padlock, she asked this Gates Foster, "Would you be so kind as to bring me my pills? The ones next to the knife." The ones on the cloisonné plate she indicated with a trembling finger. She lay back and told him, "I don't want to be here when this happens."

His face so pale he almost glowed against the dark smoke, he asked, "Are you in labor?"

Mitzi tumbled the pills into her mouth and chewed them. Choked them down with wine. Said, "I killed your child. Lucinda."

He looked at the knife on the mixing console and said, "I can't."

Mitzi reached out and clutched at the microphones, drawing them close like old friends. She reached up and pulled the hanging mics until they hovered in her face. She said, "Lucinda. Your Lucy was lost in a building, down town." Her words smearing and dissolving. "I found her.

She'd always wanted an older sister." She lifted her head to meet his eyes as she said, "I stabbed her to death on this very table." The needles on the meters jumped in unison.

Gates Foster, this father who'd waited all these years to come here, his face begged her for a different truth. Then he picked up the knife.

Foster listened. She'd done one thing wrong, she said. She explained that it only takes one prick, one slice of a knife to start someone screaming but a hundred more to make it stop. She'd spent her whole life trying to resolve the afternoon she'd brought one little girl home.

He couldn't. Not at first. He said, "You're lying." He said Lucinda wasn't dead. This Mitzi person was his last link to her. He'd arrived here after seventeen years of slogging through the underworld where people fucked children and murdered them. He only picked up the knife to threaten her, but now the images hit him. The inventory of brutalized children. The hurricane of screams and smoke churned around him until one scream began to loop, screaming, "Help me! Daddy, please, no! Help me!"

The Mitzi person looked up at him, and he knew it was true. He had nothing more to discover. Nothing was worth more asking. She wore a loose-fitting smock, and he worried the knife might ruin it. An absurd thought. It was a movie. He told himself he was in a movie. And Foster swung his arm like planting a flag.

* * *

The knife drove into Mitzi's chest with steady thuds. Withdrew and drove in. Withdrew with the perfect sucking sound she was so careful to include in jobs. A peace, the peace of shock and trauma had settled over her body and mind. Something more profound than the oblivion of wine and Ambien.

Now would come the hundred wounds to resolve the first, and he stabbed her again. He was sobbing. Her blood and his own tears mixed with soot on his face, a mask of red and black.

A small girl stood off to one side of the table and said, "Mitzi, I'm here. I'm going to help you get home."

The girl cast pitiful eyes on her father, and Mitzi told her, "He can't see you." Her voice jumped as the Foster person yanked the knife out and stood ready to plunge it in again.

The girl, Lucinda, Lucy, her little sister for just one day, said, "Tell him about the pot roast. Tell him about cutting the end off with a big knife."

As the knife came down, Mitzi stammered the strange message, and the blade stopped short of entering her chest.

Lucinda cried out, "Tell him that Grandma Linda is here with me."

Mitzi gasped out the message.

"Tell him," Lucinda cried, "that this wasn't his fault."

Mitzi tasted blood. Blood bubbling up from her lungs,

and as she coughed and gasped to speak, specks of this blood peppered the microphones that clustered close to hear her. The needles jumped on the meters, but only faintly, before settling back to rest. She couldn't speak, but she could hear. She could no longer feel the chains binding her legs together. She could no longer see, not out of her own eyes, but she could feel a small hand close around hers and hear Lucinda's voice say, "Come with me. I know you're lost. I'll take you home."

A second figure stepped out of the smoke. A dumpy man wearing a tuxedo. Malachite cuff links he had on. A Timex watch he wore around one hairy wrist and a sweet-smelling gardenia in his lapel. With him was a woman Mitzi had only seen in photographs. Mitzi's bloodless face smiled. "Schlo. You look good…"

Schlo smiled in return. "Baby girl, I wish I could say the same for you." He beckoned for her to get up and come along with him. He glanced fondly at the woman accompanying him. A blonde. He said, "Your mother would very much like to meet you."

Foster continued to stab. The recorded screams continued, but she was dead. She was dead, but Foster couldn't stop. He'd no idea how to do what needed to be done, so he sliced and hacked. He was chopping open a rosewood coffin. He tore aside the shredded, sodden clothes and dug into her and felt among the sticky, cooling organs of her.

He entered her. Entered and defiled. Defiled and destroyed as he rummaged through her the way he'd hunted through so many miles of tape, through so many websites, scrambling through the slippery contents of her body. With his bare hands he clawed with fingernails rimed in gore, and his fingers found what he'd hoped.

As the power failed, the lights failed. In a scene lit only by the crackling, flashing, orange flames, the screams grew quiet as reels slowed to stop. And as the last scream faded, Foster lifted his dripping prize from the dead woman. It took its first breath from the toxic air and began to wail. And the scream of that child brought into this sweltering, polluted, dark world, its voice surpassed all the screams of those people leaving it.

The slamming against the front door had stopped. But as the child cried in his arms, a new sound began. A buzzing. The buzzer that meant someone at the street door. If he'd die here or die at the hands of those outside, he'd little choice. Blinded by the fire, Foster carried the blood-sticky, shivering infant boy up the stairs to where he fumbled with the locks and threw the door open.

On the street stood a solitary figure. No army. No police. Only a woman with a limousine parked near her. In the lapse between the retreating mercenaries and the approaching fire engines, there was just this woman. She said, "You have a baby."

She wore a gleaming double strand of natural pearls around her neck.

He offered the child, and Blush Gentry took it into her arms.

As if just by joining forces, every Pomeranian and Chihuahua in the neighborhood, every corgi and dachshund in the city, they howled to manifest a siren. The siren created the flashing strobes of red and blue. The lights brought the first fire engine. Their combined voices conjured a second, a third, and a fourth, but it was too late. Flames exploded through the roof of Ives Foley Arts. Flames roared from the street door left ajar.

Inside, flaming microphones drooped on their stands. Suspended mics dropped from the ceiling. In the prop room the axes burned, the ice picks and Bowie knives and bludgeons burned. The flames, fed by the endless lengths of magnetic tape. Wires melted. Meters ticked as if monitoring their own death.

In this, these final moments, a reel found the power to turn. A tape began to play and the sound issued from the last small speaker. A little girl said, "Close your eyes. Listen and guess."

A gentle sound followed, a soft pattering noise.

Another girl cried out, "Rain!"

The older girl said, "Now tell me what you had for breakfast, Lucy."

The younger said, "Cheerios. Scrambled egg. A glass of milk."

A door opened and closed, footsteps. A man's voice said, "Mitzi, who's your new friend?"

The older girl said, "Lucy, I'd like you to meet my father."

And at this, the last tape began to melt and burn.

On the television a young woman was tied to an elaborate brass bed in a dingy log cabin. A mob of Confederate soldiers crowded into the room, one among them holding a carving knife. Another asked, "Are you going to tell us where them slaves is hid, Tammie Belle, or are we gonna have to execution you?"

Gates sat on a sofa eating popcorn from a bowl in his lap. Beside him Blush held their son, Lawton.

The soldiers attacked the woman, and she screamed. At least a scream occurred, clearly dubbed in. Gates Foster clicked to another channel. There, there was not-Lucinda. She was television's newest discovery, Meredith Marshall, playing the lead in a sitcom about a wisecracking father and daughter who ran a detective agency. The man playing her father was not-Robb Laurence. Just two of the entirely new generation of film and television stars, their ratings were stellar.

A laugh track roared after every line of dialogue.

As he chewed popcorn, Foster asked himself if anything was real in the world. Anything or anyone. Even the popcorn didn't taste right. He clicked back to the Civil War flick. He said, "This movie is terrible."

The baby woke and began to fuss. Blush hushed the child, saying, "The scream was good."

Her husband didn't reply. He checked his emails, holding the phone so his wife couldn't see. And opened the one from the Idaho Department of Statistics, reading it not for the first time that day. Not even the tenth time. He'd learned it by heart. In summary, the state records showed that no Lawton Koestler had ever been registered in any Idaho school. No birth certificate had ever been issued for a child with that name. No boy had ever died of a peanut allergy, died clutching the hand of a future movie star atop a chilly mountain while menaced by wild cats.

Idaho didn't even have a fucking Beech Mountain.

Blush Gentry, or whoever she was, she'd made it up. Played him like a fish and reeled him in. Or the story had been taught to her by whoever had trained Robb, the same party who'd staged the fake support group and taunted Foster at the fake funeral they'd held. Whatever deep state operation, it had funneled the child abuse pictures to him. To stoke his rage for their own purpose.

When he'd been mired in despair, the operation had sent him the video of Lucinda's scream.

Foster crammed his mouth with popcorn and wiped his greasy fingers on the sofa cushion. His rage wasn't gone.

It only needed a refresh.

For this he scrolled through his gallery of monsters. If his guess was correct, he could have his pick, now. The people he chose from the dark web, they would be delivered to him like pizzas for him to do with as he pleased. Like meat to be bled or carved or burned.

It would be healing.

Granted, his methods weren't perfect. Mistakes would be made. But even the innocent dead wouldn't suffer in vain. There was that. Foster could conduct his interrogations and vent his frustrations. And, if nothing else, motion pictures would see an improvement.

Foster looked at his beautiful wife—whoever she was. He looked at their baby—the offspring of strangers. One day this boy, his own son would follow in his footsteps.

Gates Foster would never be stopped because he worked for the people who did the stopping. Likewise, he would never be caught.

His future looked simple. Simple and bright. Bright and bottomless.

ABOUT THE AUTHOR

CHUCK PALAHNIUK has been a nationally bestselling author since his first novel, 1996's *Fight Club*, was made into the acclaimed David Fincher film of the same name. Palahniuk's work has sold millions of copies worldwide. He lives outside Portland, Oregon.